King of the Trap 2

Lock Down Publications and Ca$h
Presents
King of the Trap 2
A Novel by *T.J. Edwards*

Lock Down Publications
P.O. Box 944
Stockbridge, Ga 30281

Visit our website @
www.lockdownpublications.com

Copyright 2021 T.J. Edwards
King of the Trap 2

First Edition April 2021
Printed in the United States of America

This is a work of fiction. Names, characters, places, and incidents either are products of the author's imagination or are used fictitiously. Any similarity to actual events or locales or persons, living or dead, is entirely coincidental.

Lock Down Publications
Like our page on Facebook: Lock Down
Publications @
www.facebook.com/lockdownpublications.ldp
Cover design and layout by: **Dynasty Cover Me**
Book interior design by: **Shawn Walker**
Edited by: **Lashonda Johnson**

Stay Connected with Us!

Text **LOCKDOWN** to 22828 to stay up-to-date with new releases, sneak peaks, contests and more...
Thank you.

Submission Guideline.

Submit the first three chapters of your completed manuscript to ldpsubmissions@gmail.com, subject line: Your book's title. The manuscript must be in a .doc file and sent as an attachment. Document should be in Times New Roman, double spaced and in size 12 font. Also, provide your synopsis and full contact information. If sending multiple submissions, they must each be in a separate email.

Have a story but no way to send it electronically? You can still submit to LDP/Ca$h Presents. Send in the first three chapters, written or typed, of your completed manuscript to:

LDP: Submissions Dept
P.O. Box 944
Stockbridge, Ga 30281

DO NOT send original manuscript. Must be a duplicate.

Provide your synopsis and a cover letter containing your full contact information.

Thanks for considering LDP and Ca$h Presents.

T.J. Edwards

Chapter 1

It was a week after we recovered Odana from her captives. Maze hit my phone at 5:00 in the morning from the county jail saying that he needed me to come pick him up. He'd gotten pulled over coming back from Staten Island. The police found a few stuffed blunts inside his ashtray, along with a bottle of Oxycontin. He was supposed to wait for a bail hearing but due to the fact that it was a nonviolent offense, and the jails were overcrowded, they were letting him go with a hefty fine. I agreed to come and get him even though I was groggy as ever this morning.

Me and Ashlynn had spent the whole night talking and getting to know each other on a higher level. Now that she was set to have my child, I wanted to really understand who she was as a woman. So, we talked, and then when our mouths became so dry that we needed water to replenish them we talked some more. When we finally passed out it was 4:30 in the morning. So, at 5:30 when Maze called me, I wanted to punch somebody.

Ashlynn rolled over in the bed and grabbed the clock off the night table while I was up getting dressed. Odana was already up and watching the big screen without any sound. She had the caption going across the bottom of it.

Ashlynn looked at the clock with her face scrunched up. "What is going on? Why are you up so early making all that noise?"

"I gotta go out for a minute. My nigga Maze gotta get picked up from the county jail. They're releasing him. I'll be right back. I just gotta go over to Staten Island."

"What?" Ashlynn sat up in bed and the covers fell off her exposing her naked breasts. "I'm supposed to believe that you are going to pick him up and not meet up with Tasia or somebody else. Yeah, the fuck right."

I frowned. "Yo,' we just sat here for the last week having the best conversations ever. I thought we were getting a clear understanding. What, you still don't trust me or something?" I slipped my shirt over my head and grabbed my car keys.

I thought about grabbing my pistol too but the police were pulling everybody over and asking them where they were going, and when they would return home because the Governor of New York had put out a stay-at-home order for the entire state until the Coronavirus pandemic was over. I didn't want to get caught up in no bullshit, so I decided against the idea.

"Yeah, I trust you alright. I trust you so much that I am about to send Odana with you. She ain't doing shit anyway, besides that is your sister-in-law. Y'all need to get to know each other. Get up, Odana and go with him."

Odana pulled the sheet off her and stood up in just her bra and panties. She began to get dressed. "How do we know that Garvey and the Deadly Guerillas aren't looking for me all over New York? What if they catch us out there and kill the both of us?"

"That's nonsense. Me and King already talked. You are going to be safe. I am pregnant. That's all King ever asked for. Besides, Garvey is too busy warring with King's army to worry about a prisoner. Y'all just need to go and come back," Ashlynn ordered.

"Aw man, why can't you just go? He's your husband." Odana shot the evil eye at her sister.

"Because you are going, and that's final. I got something I gotta do." Ashlynn stood up naked. She picked up her panties that were on the side of the bed and slipped them on. "Hurry up and go so y'all can get back. Oh, and while you're out

Tyson, pick up these few items for me." She grabbed her phone and texted me a list of things to grab from Walmart.

I read my phone and wanted to curse her ass out. "Yo', I ain't fuckin wit Walmart, right now. The lines are wrapped around the block. Plus, early in the morning like this, they ain't letting nobody in but senior citizens."

"Well, I need every item on that list, so—" She walked up the stairs. "Make it happen." She disappeared.

I read over my phone. "Man, it's gon' take us all day to get this shit. Come on."

***

Odana turned down the Griselda track that I was bumping out of my speakers and looked over at me. She had to move her long, reddish, curly hair out of her face because she had the window slightly rolled down and it was blowing it everywhere.

"I never did get a chance to tell you that I appreciate you for helping my sister get me out of that jam. You have no idea what those men were getting ready to do to me." She shook her head. "But seriously though, thank you."

I looked over at her and smiled. "It's all good. I'm just glad that you are safe." I went back to looking at the road.

The scent of Odana's perfume was filling up the interiors of the car. I was trying my best to not pay attention to how fine she was. Though she and Ashlynn had a lot of similarities Odana was darker and had just a tad bit more weight on her. Her eyes were ocean blue, and she seemed very quiet and laid back.

"So, what's the deal with you and my sister anyway? Are you two working things out?" She rested her arm on the window seal.

"We are a work in process, but now that she is getting ready to have my child I gotta get my shit together. It's good, though."

"Yeah. Well, I don't really know you like that, but you seem like a really good man. You two will figure it out. It takes time." She patted my right leg and squeezed it, then she went back to looking out her window.

I would be lying if I said that what she'd just done didn't make me feel a way, but I pushed all those thoughts out of my mind quickly. Odana was my baby mother's sister. There was no way I would ever think about crossing that line. I was better than that.

"Plus, you're fine, too. I'll give Ashlynn that. She got a fine ass husband. Y'all will be alright."

I glanced over at her. "Yeah, we will be." Then I laughed to myself with all kinds of crazy thoughts going through my mind.

***

"Yo' Kid, it was mad disgusting up in there. They had mafuckas coming in there all kinds of sick. It's no wonder they were letting people off with a slap on the wrist. That Coronavirus shit is bad news. Who is shorty right here, she's gorgeous?" Maze got into the back seat and closed the door.

"This my lil sister, Odana. She's from Jamaica."

Maze held out his hand. "Nice to meet you little, Miss Jamaica. How can I get to know you on a deeper level?"

She shook his hand and frowned. "I'm not interested but thank you for the compliment."

"Yo' ma, I don't know how yo' people get it in down there where you're from, but I'm from Brooklyn. I get mad chips. You gimme the time of day and I'ma change ya life. Word up." He kissed the back of her hand.

"Still not interested but thank you." She pulled her hand away from him and bucked her eyes at me. "I'm supposed to be ya sister and this is how you protect me? Really?"

I laughed. "Maze is good people. He don't mean no harm." My phone buzzed. I picked it up and placed it to my ear. "What it do?"

"Tyson, please help me."

I eased my foot off the gas and pulled to the side of the road. "Who dis?"

"It's Tasia, he's trying to kill me. He's in there beating the hell out of my mother. She's trying to stop him from getting to me. He swears that he wants me dead. Please help me."

"Who the fuck is doing this?" I snapped, hitting a U-turn heading toward Ms. Jazzy's house.

"Kammron, he's fucked up off drugs and alcohol. Please don't let him kill me," she whimpered.

"You're at your mother's house out in Brooklyn, right?" I asked, stepping on the gas a little more.

"Yeah, please hurry!" I could hear the beating on the door in the background, and then a loud bang. "Leave my mama alone, daddy. Please leave her alone! Arrgh!" The phone went dead.

"Hello? Hello? Tasia? Tasia? Fuck!" I hung up and placed the phone on my lap.

"Yo' what the fuck was all that about?" Maze asked, leaning over my seat.

"My sister told me to be on high alert for a bitch named Tasia. I take it, that was her?" Odana raised her right eyebrow.

"Tasia's daddy tripping. This nigga is trying to kill her and Ms. Jazzy. I gotta get over there right away." I jumped on the highway.

"Fine ass Ms. Jazzy with the ass and body? Her nigga?" Maze shook his head and sighed loudly. "You betta have a pistol in dis mafucka if you talking about Kammron from Harlem. That nigga is crazy, and he stays wit' them hammers like he a Carpenter or somethin'."

"Yeah, I'm talking 'bout that nigga, but n'all I ain't got no pistol in here. I gotta stop at the crib real fast."

I sped all the way to Brooklyn and was surprised that I didn't get pulled over by the law. There were very few people out. When I pulled up to my parent's home, I parked the car and rushed up on the stoop. My mother's car was gone. For a split second, I wondered where she could have gone but then remembered her being called into work that morning because she was a registered nurse, and they were short on staff at the small hospital that she worked at because a lot of the nurses kept getting sick. Hermés was sitting on the stoop with a black hood pulled over her head smoking a cigarette. She flicked it when I got to the top step. There were dark bags under her eyes.

She stood up and held out her hands. "Tyson, I shoulda kept shit real with you in the beginning but I just didn't know how to."

I was in a frenzy. "Sis, I wanna holler at you but not right now. I gotta get in here and grab somethin' when I get back you and I need to talk, okay?"

She held me for a second. "Just know that I wanted to tell you that it was never about you. I love you, go in there." She kissed my cheek.

I looked at her funny and then rushed into the house. I ran into the kitchen and directly to the back door. I pulled it open and hurried down the stairs knowing that time was of the essence when I hopped off the last step, I almost had a heart attack from the sight before. There in the middle of the bed was Ashlynn. She was butt naked, moaning at the top of her lungs while my father King fucked her like a savage with her legs on top of his shoulders. When Ashlynn looked up and saw me, she tried to push King off her. His hips slammed into her back-to-back before he growled and shuddered while hugging her close to his body.

I laughed. "Yeah?"

King turned around and when he saw me his eyes got big. He slipped out of her and stood before me with his piece shining with her juices on it. "Son, I kin' explain."

I grabbed my gun and headed back toward the steps. "I ain't trippin'. Do what y'all do. All I wanna know is if that baby she is carrying is mine or yours?"

Ashlynn pulled the sheet around her body tighter. She looked over at King. "Are you going to tell him what's really going on, or am I?"

My phone started to buzz again. Tasia's face came across it. My mother appeared at the top of the stairs with a knife in her hand. Hermés looked over her shoulder. Ashlynn backed away and picked up a knife of her own.

Chapter 2

"So, are you going to tell him what's going on, or am I?" Ashlynn said and slipped from the bed searching for her under clothes. She picked up her discarded panties and began to get into them.

"Nah, Shorty, y'all ain't gotta tell me shit. I don't give a fuck. Next time I worry about what's going on wit' you, it will be when you pop that kid out, until then, you're King's problem." I turned my back on the pair trying to decide if they had me feeling a way?

The image of my father fucking the shit out of my wife was going to be permanently burned into my brain for the rest of my life. That was one thing I knew for sure. I turned around to face them, ready to say something, that I hadn't even made up my mind as to what it was going to be just yet.

Before I could open my mouth, my father, King spoke up, "Tyson, come ear', and lissen' to what I gotta say. Ya don't unda' stand dee' importance of a chile' tween' you and Ashlynn, ya' need to ear' me out 'bout dee' matter'." He slipped into his boxers and took a step toward me.

"Yeah, Tyson, please just listen to what your father has to say. Once you see things more clearly, you'll probably understand what has to take place in order to fulfill the legacy. Trust me, baby, this thing is bigger than the both of us."

"Yo, I said what I said. Far as I'm concerned, that marriage shit is a sham. I don't give a fuck about Ashlynn, Jamaica, the legacy, or none of that shit. I ain't even feeling you like that, Shorty. So, I hope that kid ain't mine because I don't want no parts of none of this. I'm out."

King quick as a deadly Cheetah blocked my path. He stood before me with his nostrils flared, and thick veins coursing through his neck. He flexed his fingers over and over. "Ya' tink' mu' sun' gonna' defy mi orders and livv'ta' tell 'bout dis'. Ya tick' to dee legacy or mi disown you." He pointed at me. "You fend fa ya' self and die in dee' jungle without meh. Go out dat' damn door and no blood of dee' great King any longer. Mi allows death to come." He licked his thumb and traced across my forehead.

I slapped his hand away. "Fuck you! I spit on your legacy." I spit onto the concrete. "That bitch is your problem, and so is Jamrock. I'm out." I turned my back and left the basement with him swearing at the top of his lungs that I was going to die and that he was officially disowning me.

I didn't care. I felt like I no longer needed him, and I didn't want to be under his umbrella any longer. I didn't fully understand what consequences I was about to be faced with, but I did get the fact that as soon as I turned my back on, King. I was basically choosing to walk into the valley of death, and I was a bit fearful, and cool with that at the same time.

When I got to the top of the stairs, my mother, Amanda was waiting for me with tears in her eyes and two duffel bags. She wiped her eyes and took a hold of my shoulders. She looked me in the eyes. "Run son, run away, and be your own man. This Jamrock life was never meant for you. I see it now, so go. Go far away from here, and don't allow your father to catch you because he is going to try and kill you. You are already marked by so many for death." She squeezed her eyelids and more tears sailed down her cheeks.

I pulled her to me and tried to wrap my arms around her. She stopped me and shook her head. "No, there is no time for softness, nor weaknesses. Take these bags and become great. Your father, King is your number one enemy now, trust me. Go." She pushed me in the chest as if she were a bully in the school yard. More tears fell down her cheeks.

I stumbled back. "Mama, hug me. One last hug, please." I walked up to her with my arms open just wide enough for her small frame.

She slapped my hands away. "Go! Now! Go, or I swear I will kill you myself." She took a step back and pulled one of the machetes off the wall that we had there along with another. The two had formed the letter X. "Don't make me do this, son." She raised the machete over her head, ready to swing.

I backed up. "But mama, I love you," My voice began to crack. "Mama, let me hug you."

"No emotions!" She swung the machete. I could feel the blade whip past my cheek. "The next time I slay you."

I jumped back, picked up the two duffel bags, and nodded my head. "Okay, then, if that's the way you want it." Tears fell down my cheek. "I'm out of here." I turned and left, but before I did, I looked over my shoulder and she was on her knees rocking back and forth, crying her eyes out.

I rushed out of the house, and down the stairs. Hermes stood up, she flicked a cigarette into the grass and ran her hand over her face. "Baby brother, did you see them? Did you catch, Daddy, wit that Jamaican bitch?"

I opened the back door of my Camaro. "Yeah, I saw them, and I'm glad I did. I ain't fuckin' with dude no more. He can't tell me what to do. I'm outta this bitch, and from under his thumb."

Hermes shook her head. "No, you can't do that. He's going to kill you."

I stuffed the bags all the way onto the back seat and shrugged my shoulders. "Then let him kill me. I'd rather die free than let dude run my life for the rest of my life. Are you coming with me?"

She shook her head. "No, I'm not ready to die, and besides, if I stay here then at least I will be able to know what he's planning against you. You should be careful. I love you with all of my heart."

Before a tear dropped from her eyes, I had the engine roaring on my Camaro. Odana jumped out and ran into the house, and I smashed away from the curb with anger and intense hatred for my father brewing inside me.

***

"Yo, Kid, I know you steaming, right now, and it's impossible for you to think logically. But are you sure you wanna do this shit? That nigga, King is bananas, B. Son got mob ties all over Jamaica. I ain't talking no weak wimpy ass mafuckas' neither. I'm talking the kind of assassins that murder shit before they even eat breakfast," Maze said adjusting the Tech-9 on his lap.

"I don't care about none of that. Fuck my pops, kid, word up. My whole life he has been telling me what to do, and how to do it. I'm over that shit. I don't understand anything about that Jamaican legacy shit, and I don't want to. I'm my own man, and I wanna get this shit out the mud on my own terms." I sped off the Expressway and slowed the car as I came to the lights.

My head was spinning, and the only person I could really think about was Tasia. I was praying that I could get to her before Kammron did anything serious to her.

Maze leaned forward and nodded his head. "Alright den, Dunn, you already know that I'm fuckin' wit you until the bitter end. If you are about to go rogue, it's gon' be a bunch of drama and shit that comes along with it, but I'ma hold you down. That's my word. We gon' have to mount up, though, gotta be strapped, and manned up." He frowned.

I looked over at him as I pulled through the lights. "I'm wit' it. You already know I ain't as well versed in the streets as you are, but that mob shit runs deep in my veins. I'ma follow yo' lead until my instincts kick in. Once that shit happens, it's gon' be hell to pay the captain."

Maze laughed. "Son, if you ever wind up turning into your father the whole world gon' have to pay the captain." He laughed again. "All I know is that we gon' have to get shit up and running real fast before he comes for you. I can tell that by the way, your sister was looking. She is worried about what your old man is going to do to you. She had bags all under her eyes and shit. That ain't nothing but stress right there." He shook his head.

And heroin, I thought.

My heart was still torn in two after finding out that Hermes had tried the drug and appeared to be using it on a regular basis, to cope with life. I always thought my sister was stronger than that, but then again, New York City had a way of getting a man or woman down. Life to me was an angry bitch on her period.

***

When I pulled up in front of Tasia's home, her mother, Jazzy was coming down the stairs with tears running down her cheeks. She looked back at the walkup apartment where they stayed and wound up falling down the last row of steps. She got up and proceeded to jog down the block. She appeared distraught, and grief-stricken.

I opened the door and ran over to meet her. The .40 Glock felt heavy in my lower back. I grabbed her by the shoulders. It seemed as if it took her a second to recognize that it was me because at first, she froze and closed her eyes.

"Jazzy, what's the matter? Where is Tasia?"

She shook her head. "He gon' kill my baby. That man gon' kill my baby, and it's all my fault!" she screamed.

People began to come out of their apartments to see what all the commotion was about.

"Who finna' kill, Tasia? Where is she?" I shook her, becoming impatient.

"K-K-Kammron, I shoulda gotten away from him the first time I caught those two together. But when a man pays all your bills, you feel so lost, so dependent, so stupid."

I didn't want to hear that shit. I needed to know where Tasia was. "Is she still upstairs? Tell me and quit all this mafuckin' rambling!" I tightened my grip on her shoulders. I shook her again. "Is she upstairs?"

"Yeah, she is. She is, baby, but so is he. You don't wanna get involved with Kammron. That nigga is crazy. Ask anybody. I gotta just allow this situation to play itself out."

"What, and that's your daughter?" I flung her ass to the side and headed up the steps to her apartment with Maze right behind me.

Once inside of the walk up's main door, I hurried up the stairs inside the building three at a time until I was standing outside of Jazzy's door. I tried the knob and pushed it inward. The door fell open, and I made haste inside. I could hear the sounds of a struggle.

"Please, Kammron! Get off me! I can't take no more! Please, man, have mercy on me!" Tasia screamed.

"Bitch, be still!" Kammron roared.

"Please!" Tasia hollered again.

"Be still, or I'ma blow yo' mafuckin' head off," Kammron promised.

I had heard all I needed to. I came in front of the bedroom door and lifted my foot, and with one hard kick, it flew open. The door landed against the wall and fell part way off its hinges. There was Kammron, straddled on top of Tasia with his hands around her neck choking her while he fucked her hard. Sweat dripped off his face. He turned around to see who had kicked in the door, by the time he recognized that he was being invaded I was slamming the handle of the pistol along the side of his forehead and knocking him off the bed.

"Bitch ass nigga! Get the fuck off my bitch!" I hollered.

He fell onto his side and laid there for a moment. His eyes were closed. He grimaced in pain. Then he slowly opened them and brought his fingers up to the split in his skin that leaked his blood.

"No, the fuck you didn't attack the god." He came to his knees.

Tasia had already rushed behind me. She struggled to put her panties and clothes on. "He got a gun under the bed, Tyson. Don't let him get to that gun."

I ran and kicked him as hard I could in the ribs. He flipped over. I aimed my pistol down at him. "Bitch nigga, you in here raping my, shorty, huh?" I cocked the hammer.

Kammron came to his knees and held his hands up. "Alright, alright." His forehead continued to leak blood. "Now, I know this shit might look real crazy because she was hollering and all that shit, but this is what you call role-playing lil' homie. She liked this shit."

"You're a liar!" Tasia screamed.

Kammron pointed at her. "Bitch, act like you tough and I'll kill you. Now you already know what this is. Clearly this nigga don't." He eyed me and came to his feet. "So, now what? You gon' ice me over a bitch, huh? That's the title you want? You wanna be that nigga that killed Kammron the great over a shot of pussy? Really? I got a hunnit gees say you let me walk out this bitch."

"Bet, where that cash at?" Maze said, stepping forward with two Desert Eagles drawn.

Kammron lowered his eyes. "Maze, from Red Hook? Nigga I just dropped yo' uncle off twenty birds for the buildings. Tell this lil' nigga to stall me out, and that cash is yours, word is bond." He smiled sinisterly.

"Don't listen to him, Tyson. Kammron is crazy. If you let him walk out of here, he is going to kill you and me. Don't nobody ever touch him and live to tell about it. Shoot him. Shoot him now!" Tasia warned.

"You stupid bitch, you gon' tell yo' nigga to shoot me!" Kammron lashed out at Tasia and leaped over the bed.

I don't know why I did it, or how I allowed myself to get sucked in so deeply, but as soon as he jumped in the air I got to bussing. *Boom! Boom! Boom! Boom!*

The bullets ripped into his flesh and sent him flying backward. He fell to the floor bloody and curled into a ball. The next thing I knew he was laid out flat on his back, with blood leaking out of him.

"Holy fuck, my nigga. You smoked, Killa Kamm, Harlem's King of the trap." Maze had moved me out of the way so he could see the predicament of Kammron more clearly.

"Let's get out of here. Please, let's get out of here," Tasia said again. Her eyes were bucked wide open, and she looked sick on the stomach.

I held the smoking gun. I stood over, Kammron, and looked down at his bitch ass. In my opinion, when a dude did a female the way that he'd done, Tasia that was the fate he was supposed to have gotten. I felt my actions were necessary to clear out fuck niggas like him.

"Yeah, let's get up out of this bitch."

We broke up out of the house, and headed down the stairs, just as Jazzy was coming back up them. Her mascara was in streaks all over her face. She stopped, and almost blocked us from getting out of the front door. "What happened up there? I heard a gunshot. What did you do?" she asked this question looking directly at, Tasia.

"What did I do? What do you mean, what did I do? What did Kammron do to me, mama? And what has he *been* doing? That should be your question."

"Not now." Jazzy slung her out of the way and took the stairs two at a time. We waited until she screamed, "Oh, my God." Before we rushed to hop into my Camaro, and storm away from the scene.

T.J. Edwards

Chapter 3

Six Months Later

"Damn, it's so hot in here. I thought you said they were coming to fix that air conditioner today?" Tasia asked, as she licked her thumb, and started to count the stack of twenty-dollar bills that were in front of her.

Maze came into the apartment and placed a duffel bag on the table in front of me. "Here, bruh, that Grenada dog food rocking like a mafucka all over Brooklyn. If shit keeps moving like this, we gon' fuck' around and have enough money to cop us those tools that we need to take over the Red Hook houses. The lil' young niggas we got running under us is hollering that they are, King Tyson crazy. We only been at this shit for four months going hard now." Maze plopped into the chair across from mine.

"That's how you know those lil' niggas ain't loyal to us, and that they are loyal to the money. A mafucka can walk up to me and knock my shit loose, take over the operations that we got going and those lil' dudes will be hollering that he is the king and that they are running under him. That's why this shit is a business to me, and nothing more." I kept breaking down the Grenadian Heroin that my mother had me plugged with and copping from her native land.

Ever since I'd fallen out with King she'd found a way to help me to heavily cement myself within the deadly trenches of New York City where the money was fast and as dirty as it got.

"Fuck you think I'ma do if a nigga knocks yo' head off? You honestly think I ain't gon' kill everything and everybody that he's close to?" Maze asked with a mug on his face.

25

I took the kilo of Heroin and stabbed a screw driver directly into the center of it, before turning my wrist left and right to create a break inside it. Once it broke off into chunks, I was able to weigh it up and distribute it accordingly throughout Brooklyn.

"You betta, cause you already know I'd do the same for you."

"Baby, the air conditioner. When are you getting it fixed?" Tasia asked, wiping sweat from her brow.

"Shorty, this is the trap. This mafucka is supposed to be hot, and uncomfortable." Maze laughed. "You know she green to this shit. She asking about air conditioning in a Bando." He shook his head.

Tasia rolled her eyes. "Look, Maze, why you always got something stupid to say, especially when I ain't talking to you? Damn, why can't you mind yo' own business sometimes?"

"That's my nigga. My right muthafuckin' hand. Sometimes before he can even get the words out, I do, and that's how shit goes. I know you might be feeling some type of way about that, but you'll be alright'. This is the trap, fuck air conditioning."

Tasia slammed the money down on the table so hard that the headscarf she had wrapped around her head came a bit undone. "Yo', you see how he talking to me, Tyson? I'm supposed to be ya Whiz. Dis' how you let this stud talk to me, though?"

"Yo', y'all leave me out of that childish ass shit. I'll go snatch up an air conditioner later today. For now, keep counting that money because I'ma need a grand total before five o'clock. That's what time we meeting up with Bonkers, right?"

Maze nodded. "Yeah, the homie says he got some nice M90s for the crew. He also said that Kammron is still in a coma out in D.C. He'd come out of it three days ago and fell right back into it. One day he strong, and the next he is weak as an old lady."

"I fucked up. I thought I smoked that nigga," I said out loud while separating four big chunks that I was set to break down into smaller pieces.

"Yeah, Dunn, whenever that nigga do wake all the way up, we gotta hope he don't remember what the deal is. Long as his memory is shot, we should be good, cause Ms. Jazzy ain't saying nothing. I still think we should ice her ass, though," Maze said this last part under his breath, but I was still able to make out what he was saying.

"You see what I'm saying, Tyson. It's like this nigga be just saying shit to get a rise out of me. Now he talking about killing my mother. Where does it end?" Tasia snapped mugging Maze.

"Yo', dis' is the game, Shorty. And in the game, a mafucka can't be all soft and worried about hurting a broad's feelings when business has to be handled. Your mother is the only one that knows that the homey popped, Kammron. She has information that can get all of us killed. If we smoke her and bury her ass, then we run the hopes of squashing this shit with, Kammron, too," Maze explained.

"You're not killing my mother. What the fuck is wrong with you. Tyson, can you please say something?" Tasia hollered, looking me over.

"Those mafuckin' Coke Kings, been rolling around New York for six months straight, twenty cars deep, heavily armed, and masked up, asking questions about Kammron's hit. They murdered twenty of the wrong people thinking that they had something to do with it when they didn't. Now if they'll kill twenty of the wrong people. What the fuck you think they are willing to do to three of the right people?" Maze asked her.

Tasia lowered her head. "Maze why are you always so quick to kill somebody? Why can't we send my mother off to the other side of the country? Why you gotta try and convince Tyson to give the go-ahead to have her killed?"

"Because that's how the game goes. Yo', I don't know your mother like that. I don't know how much longer she feels she can walk around holding the weight of Kammron's shooting on her heart. Every mafuckin' morning I wake up, it's nagging at me to off her ass, and keep it moving. I got bad nerves. I can't play around like that. Once she is out of the equation, we ain't got shit else to worry about," Maze said. He sat down, and unzipped the duffel bag, taking out a bundle of cash. He proceeded to count it.

"It don't matter if Ms. Jazzy says something or not. Sooner or later, I'ma have to finish that nigga. That's my bad for not doing that anyway. My pops always told me that when a 'killa' sets out to do a job that he must finish it at all costs. I shoulda never left air in that fool's lungs." I clenched my teeth and flexed my jaw muscles.

"Yeah, then I'm right, too," Maze started. "You see, once we came from out of there, any witnesses were supposed to be left slain. Clearly, we couldn't stank Tasia because she was the whole reason we went there in the first place, but Ms. Jazzy ain't have nothing to do with it. She was supposed to be a casualty of war."

Tasia hopped up and dropped the money from her hand. "That's it. Nigga, you wanna keep coming for my mama, huh?"

Maze sneered. "Yo, Tyson, get ya bitch nigga, before I show her that the only mafucka' that care about her life is you."

Tasia made her way around the table toward Maze. "Let me tell you something, Maze."

Maze hopped up and grabbed her by both of her arms. He lifted her in the air and brought her to the wall hard. "Yo', Shorty, you got me fucked up if you think you're about to come at me with that bull shit just because you fuckin' my nigga. You better get this shit through your head. He cares whether you breathe or not, I don't."

"You better get your filthy mitts off me. I don't know who you think you are!" Tasia hollered.

"What? Man, bitch." Maze raised his hand to slap her.

I caught his wrist. "Yo, Dunn, release my jewel," I said without looking at him.

He let her go. "Son, you gotta teach, shorty about the game. I ain't the mafuckin' enemy." He sat down and began to count money.

I grabbed Tasia by the wrist and took her into the back room, closing the door behind us. "Sit yo' ass on that bed."

She continued standing. "Why would you let him do me like that, Tyson. I'm supposed to be your woman," her voice began to break.

"Sit yo' ass down." I pointed at the spot where I wanted her to sit.

"Fine." She sat on the edge of the bed and crossed her arms.

"Tasia, I'ma say this one time. Then you need to just roll with the program. You aren't dealing with a bunch of average ass niggas. That fool, Maze is stomp down and a killer. His job ain't to be catering to your fuckin' feelings. You can't be jumping up, and getting all in his face, or talking that bullshit. You need to understand that you are covered only because of me."

"Covered? Man, whatever. How the hell am I covered when his black ass just had me hemmed up like a punk bitch from the street. Then on top of that, he's talking about killing my mother. What type of female would I be if I allowed him to sit around and talk about killing my fuckin' mother? And you aren't saying or doing shit." She jumped up and put her finger in my face. "I thought you had my back, Tyson. I thought you ran shit around here, but all you're doing is allowing him to run the show. This shit sucks."

I trailed my eyes up to where her finger was pointing. She got the drift and removed it. "Sit down and allow me to break something down for you."

She reluctantly sat back down. "Now what, man?"

I squatted in her face. "Do you understand what Kammron will do to your ass once he comes out of that coma, huh?"

She shrugged her shoulders. "I don't even care at this point. It seems like it doesn't matter where I am, or who I am with, I am expendable." She covered her face with both of her hands.

"Shorty, this is what a brewing war in New York looks like. Now whether you wanna keep that shit real or not. That nigga's coming to kill you as soon as he steps foot out of that hospital. As far as I know, he already has a price on yo' head and mine? What Maze was saying back there is the truth. Under any other circumstances, Jazzy is supposed to be slumped, and lifeless. The fact that she still got air in her lungs is solely because of you. But her being alive places all of our health in jeopardy."

"So, now you just wanna kill my mother just like he does. Wow, what the fuck is wrong with you two? This shit is so irritating." She rubbed her temples in a circular motion.

I took a deep breath. "Would you rather your mother be alive, or yourself?"

"Both, I don't want either one of us to die." She closed her eyes. "She's my mother, she's all I have. Can you please figure out a way where we both can be alive? Please?" She whimpered and wiped her nose.

"All I can do is my best. But right now, my main concern is you. Come here." I stood up and opened my arms for her.

She stepped into them and laid her head on my chest. I kissed the side of her forehead. She smiled and became serious again. "Tyson, I really do wanna let you know that I love you and that I appreciate you for rescuing me from that monster. I already know that you didn't have to step in and get involved, but you did it anyway and I really owe you. I hope you're not regretting your decision."

"N'all, I don't. You shoulda never had to go through no shit like that. I apologize on behalf of that nigga."

She held me tighter. "Well, I just wanted to express my gratitude. You aren't like any man that I have ever come across. I can tell that your guy doesn't like me, though, for whatever reason. I think it may be because back in the day he tried to holler at me, and I didn't give him the time of day. I was stuck on some other stuff and kinda had my head up in the clouds. It was nothin' personal."

I made her take a step back and held her small, pretty face. "We don't get off into that petty shit. Whatever you did to the homie back in the day. You best believe he ain't harboring no ill-feelings because of it. We just got a lot of shit going on and on our plate. All he knows is murder, we are making an exception for Ms. Jazzy and that's typically a no-no."

She nodded. "I know, but thank you. Personally I had to figure out how to save my mother. She doesn't need to die. She's only thirty-six years old." She hugged me again.

I wrapped my arms around her tighter. "Yeah, my word is bond. I'ma do what I can."

Chapter 4

I had never met Bonkers before, but Maze told me that both Bonkers and Kammron had been right-hand men at one point before Kammron crossed Bonkers and damn near snuffed him out. Clearly, they had a crazy history. My pops always told me that the enemy of my enemy was better off as my friend. That when it came to the trap and the game of murder, you needed to box your most powerful enemies in with enemies of their own. Well to me, Kammron was powerful. The streets of New York said he had connections that spanned all the way to the Middle East. Having pull like that, I was never supposed to try on his life, and fail with my attempt.

We pulled into the Springfield-Belmont housing projects, located in Newark, New Jersey, later that night with Maze behind the steering wheel of an all-black Land Rover. I sat in the passenger's seat with a Mach-11 on my lap and a black bandana across the lower half of my face. There were four other people in the truck. They were all young, cold-blooded, shooters from Red Hook that we'd adopted for our crew.

I had only been to New Jersey a few times, and each time I had I was used to seeing groups of niggas that looked like they were on pure bullshit. There were certain areas where they stood at stop signs and stopped you from leaving the block or entering the block for that matter until they were able to either strip you for whatever you had of value, or they were able to identify you to give you a pass. Either way, I wasn't going. If any one of those clowns thought, they were about to stop us for any reason my shooters already had the go-ahead to empty their clips. Fuck Jersey, I was a Brooklyn nigga, and I stood firm with my borough.

When we pulled into the Springfield-Belmont projects, there were about fifteen dudes crowded around the truck with handguns out.

Maze looked over at me. "Yo', kid, be smooth. That's just that fool, Bonkers' security. Ever since he and Kammron of the Coke Kings have been at war, Bonkers' beefed his security all the way up. Just chill and let these mafuckas do they once over."

"Yeah, alright, but if anything looks funny, y'all blow their ass out the way. I don't trust anything outside of us. That's including this nigga, Bonkers." I nodded my head at my shooters.

Maze cocked his F&N. "What, and you think I do. Fuck these clowns, B, word up."

Bonkers' security walked around the truck twice before they shined a flashlight inside it. Maze held up his hand and lowered the window. "Say, Money, y'all done giving us a light show or what? If you are, we got bidness to take care of wit', Bonkers."

A heavy-set, dark-skinned dude with a blue bandana around his face mugged me, then Maze, and then our shooters in the back. "You niggas got an appointment or something?"

"Yeah, bruh, he told us to pull up at eleven p.m. It's eleven o'clock on the dot, right now," I said, getting irritated. I didn't understand why my temper was getting so short lately, but it was.

"Yeah, well, the funny thing is, Bonkers forgot to relay that message to me." He eyed everybody in our truck again.

This made my levels of paranoia go all the way up. I looked back at my shooters. "Yo, so what you sayin', Dunn? You saying you ain't fuckin' wit' us or somethin'?" I slipped my hand around the handle of my Mach, ready to blast him.

Looking out the window I could see that his Homeys had the exit for the parking lot blocked off. I was ready to drop his ass.

"N'all, I ain't saying that. Just give me a second and I can hit the homie on his hip." He backed away from the truck and pulled his Tracfone out of his pocket. He turned his back to us.

"Yo', I ain't gon' lie, B, son got me nervous right now. Something about this whole thing just feels funny to me, word up," I said looking at the demeanor of the other New Jersey dudes that were blocking the exit of the big parking lot on all sides.

"N'all, Dunn, just relax. This nigga, Bonkers know what it is." Maze was thinking the same things I was, and I could tell he was second-guessing himself, even though he seemed as if he was under control.

The dude with the phone nodded his head and looked back at our truck. Then he walked further away from it and started to talk with his hands. He appeared animated, waving them around crazily.

"Yo', kid, son doing way too much talking to be getting the approval for our meeting. Fuck this shit. I say we roll up out this bitch, and look to meet up with Bonkers at another place somewhere in Brooklyn where we know what the fuck is going on? This shit got me feeling out of bounds."

Now the dude with the phone was walking off. He stopped at a group of about ten dudes, and pointed over his shoulder, with his thumb at us. They spoke for a moment. Every dude in the circle started to nod. Their faces got angrier and angrier as he spoke.

I cocked the Mach. "Get me the fuck up outta here, Maze. Right now, nigga, pull off," I ordered.

"Yo', you wilding, B. Just chill. You just don't like being outside of New York." Maze laughed.

"Blood, pull the fuck off. Now," I said again.

Maze frowned. "Tyson, chill, I'm telling you that it's all good. That fool, Bonkers would never come at us bogus."

"Bonkers knew that we were coming to buy guns, right?" I asked.

"Yeah." Maze nodded.

"And he knew we were bringing two hundred thousand, right?" Now I was antsy.

"Yeah, that's what the deal was for." Maze frowned. "Bruh, what's good?"

"Man, whose to say that Bonkers wouldn't send his lil' niggas at us for that bread, just so he could keep it on GP. You gotta think, if we're coming all the way out here for guns, he must be thinking that we ain't got none. These niggas finna' try and strip us." I scooted my seat back. "Y'all be on point back there." My shooters perked up. I lowered my window because I already knew what it was.

"Yo', now you got me 'noid' and shit." Maze sat up right. He looked over the steering wheel and eyed the building crowd.

"Man, fuck this. Get us out of here. I ain't gon' tell yo ass no more."

"Alright, nigga, we out." Maze threw the truck in drive and headed toward the exit.

As he was driving that way, the number of dudes got deeper to block the exit. By the time we pulled up to it they were every bit of thirty deep. Maze blew the horn and they didn't move. He blew it a second time. They still didn't move.

"Punch that bitch." I held the Mach out of the window and squeezed the trigger.

Doom! Doom! Doom! Doom! The Mach jumped in my hand.

The crowd of dudes began to duck for cover, so they could grab their guns and return fire.

Their bullets ate up the exteriors of our truck rocking it from side to side. The windows shattered. I kept bussing, and then my shooters joined in. Maze stepped on the gas and slammed the truck into two of Bonkers' hittas'. He kept going out of the parking lot with us shooting back at the niggas that were trying to strip us. The truck continued to take one slug after the next. We stormed down the block and made a sharp left at the end of it.

"Yo', I told you those niggas was on bullshit. I told you that something wasn't right," I snapped.

Maze kept rolling. "I just couldn't see it, B. I couldn't see that nigga, Bonkers trying to fuck us over like that."

"Why the fuck not? It's a whole ass pandemic going on. Niggas is broke and fucked up. It's a drought on the coke and the Heroin. That nigga got all those mouths to feed, and he got wind that we tried to ice, Kammron a nigga that already crushed him. He might've been thinking that we was coming to fuck him over or something. Fuck." I slammed my hand on the window seal.

Maze kept rolling. "Yo', we'll analyze that shit later until we're blue in the face. But for now, we gotta get the fuck out of this truck and into something else. There is no way we can drive back across the George Washington bridge like this. One of those toll booth mafuckas will see us and call the troopers and we got all of this money and guns in the whip."

I was steaming. "Yo', well do whatever the fuck you need to, but get me back to Brooklyn, my muthafuckin' home. I ain't never listening to you 'bout rolling out to another nigga's turf again. From here on out, if a mafucka' wanna do bidness wit' us they come to Brooklyn, or ain't shit moving."

Maze looked over at me and nodded. "Yeah, alright, Tyson. That's what it is then. But if that's gon' be the case, we gotta become more important. Right now, we ain't worthy to have mafuckas traveling to us. I'm just being honest."

***

That night, I laid in bed, with Tasia's head on my chest, and I had my eyes wide open lost in deep thought. Maze had been right about our level of importance. At that moment, we were nobodies. We were barely making a few hundred thousand a month, and by New York's standards, we were basically broke. If we wanted to be important, we were going to have to step our game all the way up. I grew angry because I came from a bloodline that was all about mass amounts of money and conquering anything and anyone in its path. I knew that I had that boss shit deep inside me, and all I would have to do was to get it to the forefront.

It was about three-thirty in the morning, and still, I lay restless with my eyes wide open. Tasia stirred in her sleep. She groaned, then kicked her legs as hard as she could, before sitting up and scooting back against the headboard. She was breathing extremely hard. She tried to swallow her spit. Then she looked down and saw that I was still awake.

I sat up. "Shorty, what's the matter with you? Why are you kicking and breathing all hard and shit?"

Tasia placed her hand over her chest, and tried to calm down, it appeared. "I keep having bad dreams about Kammron and my mother. Every night it's the same ol' thing, it's just that you aren't usually up." She took a deep breath and blew it out. "And why are you still up?"

"Don't turn shit around on me. This is what I usually do when I need to think and clear my mind. Really, I hop in my whip and just drive, but I don't feel like doing all that right now. So, I'm up. You gotta stop worrying about Kammron and believing so much in him and start respecting my gangsta. I ain't gon' allow shit to happen to you. If that was the case I would have never stepped in when I did."

Tasia shook her head. "It's not that, Tyson. I do believe in you, and I know that you have my best interests at heart. But it's also that I've been around, Kammron ever since I was a little girl. I've seen some really outlandish things. I know what he's capable of and I just hate worrying about that every single day. Plus, I don't want anything to happen to you on the account of me."

I sat up next to her and wrapped my right arm around her shoulders. "We are in this together, Tasia. I know you're scared, and that you fear the unknown, but I got you. I don't know for sure how I'm always going to be there to protect you, but I just know that I am. I don't have it all figured out, but I will in time. For now, all I ask is that you trust in me, and believe that we are going to conquer this whole Kammron situation. Do you?" I turned to look at her.

She hesitated, bit on her fingernail, and slowly shook her head. "Yeah, Tyson, I have faith and I believe in you." She laid her head on my shoulder. "I just wish all this was a dream. We're too young to be going through things like this."

"Yeah, but this is New York. Everybody in this city is forced to grow up way faster than they are supposed to, we ain't exempt. It's good, though. For as long as I have breath in my body, I am going to be there to protect you. You got my word on that."

Tasia smiled. "I've always been crazy about you, and I will always be crazy about you. You are everything." She hugged my frame, and slowly but surely, we both wound up drifting off.

Chapter 5

"Nigga, I don't know where you're getting this fire ass dog food from, but it's got the borough lit. We got fiends lined up for blocks all over Red Hook, and all they want is this same product. Yo', it's been steady for three months now, and we eating, B." Maze popped the cork on his champagne in celebration of his twentieth birthday.

We were seated in the champagne room of the 40/40 Club. It was a small and almost cramped space with two big, red, leather couches, a speaker in the upper corner of the room that played all the latest hip hop music. On the table was two buckets of ice with two bottles of champagne in each one, and a bowl of Ganja. I had two bottles of Ace of Spades in my hands, and a big blunt in my lips. I was high as gas prices, and my eyes were low.

"Don't worry about where I'm getting us right from. I got a vision, B. I gotta get up into that upper crust of the game so mafuckas can start taking us seriously. Right now, we buzzing just a lil' bit but it ain't nothing to be proud of."

"A lil' bit, nigga, please. Every time a mafucka rolls through Brooklyn, they already know who they gotta get permission from to breathe easy. Our names are building up steam real fast. The money is coming in by the droves and sooner or later we're going to be where we need to be. And, we're doing this shit without even having to fuck with Bonkers. Kid, been MIA for months now. I don't know what's good wit' him."

I sipped out of my bottle and nodded. "Yeah, I don't know what's good wit' him either, but because of that stunt he pulled back in Jersey, he gon' have to see the clan. Word up." I sat back and rested against the soft portion of the cushion. It relaxed my back muscles and made me close my eyes for a second.

Knock! Knock! Knock!

Maze jumped up and sat his bottle of liquor on the table. "Yo, this better be the entertainment, Kid, word up." Maze opened the door and frowned. "Can I help you?" He backed up and grew defensive.

Before any more words could be spoken, a tall, dark-skinned nigga with long dreads walked into the room, followed by three more dread headed men. They smelled of Old Spice and strong marijuana. The first man stopped in front of the couch where I was sitting, and his men stepped behind him. All four of them looked down on me and remained silent.

I stood up. "What's to it, blood? Why you niggas in our room?"

"The name is, Chanta. I am a member of your father's cartel. I have been assigned to bring you back into the fold by any means. Will you come home, or will you face your father's wrath?"

Maze came around and stood beside me. "How the fuck y'all even knew where we were?"

Chanta ignored him. "Speak now, Tyson, or allow me to take from this meeting what I will." He stepped forward and nearly got into my face.

I took a long swallow from my bottle and burped in his face. "That's my answer." I smiled at him.

Chanta flared his nostrils and nodded his head. "I was told to give you three chances before I killed you. You don't understand what is at stake by you going rogue. This is not the behavior of a true Prince from Jamrock.

"Yo', I don't know you niggas, but I won't hesitate to blow you niggas talking that shit to my mans like that. Ain't nobody gon' lay a finger on him, that's what that is right there," Maze said this pulling out his gun, and cocking it.

Chanta smiled. He had a mouth full of shiny gold. "Maze, your best bet is to count the days that you have left to breathe. You on the other hand do not have three chances. The longevity of your life belongs to me. If I was you, I would convince Tyson to come back into the fold. Both of you are technically too young to die."

"There go that murder talk again." I upped my .45 and put it to his forehead. His guys took a step back and appeared frozen. "Seeing as my pops told you to give me three chances before you kill me. Why don't I just whack yo' punk-ass during my first chance? That way you don't be around for the third when I tell you to kiss my black ass. How does that sound?" I cocked the hammer and pressed it harder to his forehead.

He leaned his head back and closed his eyes. "You pull that trigger, and there are more of me that's coming for you. King has conquered nearly all of Jamrock. He has bandits everywhere that's loyal to him, but a King of Jamaica can only sit comfortably, and rightfully on the throne when he has an heir sitting next to him. You are his only heir at the moment, so you must obtain your rightful place beside him."

"Or what, nigga, huh? You mafuckas think you gon' make me do some shit that I don't wanna do, huh? Fuck Jamrock, bitch ass nigga. This is Brooklyn. I don't give a fuck about you, him, or Jamrock. That shit ain't for me."

Chanta licked his lips and kept his head bent at an awkward angle. "If that is how you really feel, then you will be cursed with the plague of the island. I can only wish the best for you, but your future is dark. Now kill me in the name of the great, King Locust. Do it." He forced his forehead harder on the barrel of my gun. His three guys mugged me, yet they still didn't make a move.

"Kill his punk ass den. Smoke him. One down, three to go," Maze said this through clenched teeth.

Just then the door of the Champagne Room opened, and one of the three females screamed. "Oh, my God! Oh, my God! They are being robbed here!" The girls backed out of the room and disappeared.

Maze came and placed his hand on my shoulder. "Them bitches done seen our faces now. Come on, give that nigga a pass? We'll get up with they ass later. You better believe that." He hurried to the door and looked out of it. "Come on, Tyson."

I held my gun against his forehead for a bit longer, and then I released him. "Tell my pops that he's gotta kill me. I will never fall under him, and I don't give a fuck about Jamaica. I am my own king." I spit next to Chanta's foot.

Chanta nodded his head. "Okay, your first chance has elapsed, and I will pass this message to, King. Come on fellas." Very calmly, he and his crew made their way out of the room, and out of the club.

I sat on the couch with my gun right beside me. My head spinning like crazy. If it wasn't one thing it was another. I had to get my shit together and fast. Between Kammron, King, and Chanta sooner or later I would be exposed for the little that I had and that exposure was sure to result in the death of me if I didn't step my game all the way up.

***

Hermes pulled up to the Red Hook buildings that I was personally trapping out of later that night. When she stepped out of the car, I damned near lost my head. My sister was so skinny that I couldn't tell at first that it was her had I not caught a clear glimpse of her face. She walked up to me with her nose running, hair all over the place, and shivering as if it were below zero outside when in actuality, it was every bit of ninety degrees. She stopped in front of me and smiled weakly, one of her teeth was missing in her upper row.

I was standing beside three of my young dope boys. When I saw the state of Hermes, I became so embarrassed that I stepped away from them. I took a hold of her arm and led her to the car. "Yo', sis, you looking all kinds of crazy, right now. What's up with you?"

She gently pulled her wrist away. "Ain't nothing wrong with me. What's wrong with you? You don't look so good either." She appeared hurt.

"Look, I didn't mean to offend you. I ain't seen you in months. You lost a whole lot of weight. Why are you over here, right now?"

She shrugged her shoulders. "That's the thing, I haven't seen you in months, and I've been missing you like crazy. I felt like if I didn't get over here to Red Hook that I would never see you again. Supposedly I only got a few months to live."

Now it felt like my heart had dropped into my stomach. "Who the fuck told you that you only have a few months to live?"

"The doctors. My immune system has given up. I can't fight off anything, and I can barely keep any food down. I'm sick all the time, and I just don't know what to do. The only other option is for me to die. Shit, I welcome death." She wiped her nose with a piece of tissue from her pocket.

I found my eyes getting watery. "Sis, don't say that stupid ass shit. You ain't about to go nowhere. I don't know what's going on inside your body, but you are a fighter, and you will overcome it. All you gotta do is tell me what you need. Anything you need and I got you."

"Boy, it's too late to have me now. I'm dying, and there isn't anything anybody can do about it. This is the life that was destined for me." She dug in her dirty jean pockets and pulled out a fifty-dollar bill. "Mama, gon' kill me when she finds out I took this out of her purse." She laughed. "But here, gimme' some of that good shit that everybody has been talking about you serving."

"What?" I smacked her hand from in front of me. "You think I'm about to serve you like some fucking dope fiend?"

She smacked her lips. "Tyson, I am a dope fiend, and it's the only pleasure I have left in this life. Don't take that away from me. If I don't get it from you, I'll go over to Flatbush to get it. Either way within the next thirty minutes I'ma be high and worry-free."

I snatched her up and literally carried her all the way over to my truck that was parked halfway across the parking lot. I felt like all my niggas were looking at both her and me funny. Maze had glanced over and avoided eye contact with me a few times. Once we got to the truck, I placed her on her feet and pushed her up against the truck. "Yo', what the fuck is wrong wit' you. You calling yourself a complete dope fiend now or what?"

Hermes looked into my eyes, and then down to my hands that were holding her up against the body of my truck. "Tyson, I know I look weak, and all that. I also know that by me coming over here, and asking you to sell me some dope, after stealing the money from mama's purse makes me lower than scum, but I am still your sister and I will still muster up as much strength as I have to kick yo' ass if you don't get your filthy mitts off me." She broke my hands away from her body. "Get the fuck off me and give me what I came for now." She stumbled backward and fixed her clothes which consisted of a long T-shirt and loose-fitting black shorts. She wore Nike sandals, and one of the straps was almost all the way broken. Now tears fell out of my eyes. I wiped them away as soon as they fell. "Yo', I ain't taking ya money for no dope, Hermes. You're my mafuckin' sister, and this shit ain't happening. Get ya ass in my truck, and I'm about to feed you. I know you ain't had a good meal in only God knows how long." I reached out for her.

"Nah, nigga, I don't want no fuckin' food. I wanna get high. Do you have any idea how much pain I'm in, right now? And you're hollering this food shit?" She frowned at me. "Take the money, Tyson, and give me what I'm paying for."

"No, Shorty, that shit ain't happening. I ain't about to give you no dog food."

"Give me fifty worth, Tyson. The same shit every other addict gets. I want my Heroin strong, and I don't want to feel no more pain. Please, just give me what I got coming. I don't want to argue with you."

Yo', I was crying like a baby. I didn't give a fuck who saw me balling either. This was Hermes, my big sister, and to me the love of my whole life besides my mother. To see her broken, busted, and disgusted was fucking me up. I never thought I would see the day.

"You know what? That's alright, I'm still gon' get mine." She turned away from me. "Anybody got that Red Hook dog food! Anybody wanna make fifty dollars. All I want is five dimes. First come first serve!" she hollered.

One dope boy after the next run from seemingly everywhere to catch the money that she was attempting to spin. As soon as the first three got up to her, I was just getting out of the truck with my hand on an AR-33 assault rifle. I stepped ten feet away from her and pointed the long barrel in the sky and let that bitch ride.

Boom! Boom! Boom! Boom!

The dope boys ducked down and then took off running. I let off six more rapid shots into the air and stopped. "I catch any mafucka' in Red Hook serving my sister some mafuckin' dope, I'm whacking you on sight. That goes for everybody in this bitch, male or female. Because there were just as many dope girls serving narcotics inside Red Hook as there were boys.

Maze jogged over to me with both of his guns out. He had a red bandana over his face and Cartier glasses on his eyes. "Yo' Fleet, what the bidness, kid. You wilding, right now."

Hermes fell to the ground and sat crossed legged. She rocked back and forth as if she were in a zone. "This shit ain't right. This shit ain't cool neither. I should have never said nothing." She wiped her nose.

I stood over her. "I ain't about to lose you, Hermes. You mean too much to me for me to just let you go like that."

She shook her head. "You just don't understand. You just don't get it." She jumped up and took off running at full speed.

Maze looked as if he wanted to go after her. "What you want me to do, bruh'?"

I watched her run the length of the parking lot. Once she got to the end of it, she looked over her shoulders at me and waved me off. "I'm already dead, Tyson! You can't help me! Not you, and nobody else!" she screamed. She started jogging and ran off the block in a haste.

I slid the assault rifle back into the truck and closed the door. "Yo', I gotta clear my head, B, that sight got me all kinds of fucked up, right now. I'ma fuck wit' you in a minute." I hopped in my truck and pulled off with tears running out of my eyes, and seemingly my soul. I had never been more broken than I was at that moment.

T.J. Edwards

Chapter 6

"I know I keep sayin' it, Tyson, but I just gotta say it one more time. I am so thankful to you for copping me this Givenchy dress, and these Balenciaga heels. You got me looking like a million bucks, even though I only feel like twenty," Tasia said as she slid her arm inside mine.

We stepped onto the dance floor of Covington Night Club. It was packed, and the R&B music was blaring loud out of the speakers. She placed her face into the crux of my neck.

I took a hold of her small waist and allowed my hands to slide down to her ass. Tasia was the kind of strapped where she made both males and females feel intimidated. Males because a nigga knew that they had to be blessed in order to bed her and females because she was so fine with all of the right parts. Very few women gave her a run for her money, at least that was my opinion.

She leaned her face to the side, so she could look me in my eyes. "Did you hear what I said, Tyson? I said, thank you, for buying me these nice things and for making me feel so good about myself. I know that you're going through a lot and I wish that you would let me up into that mind of yours."

"You're welcome, Shorty, but those are just clothes. Clothes don't make the woman and it don't make a nigga a man that's buying them. When you're as stomp down, and as gorgeous as you are. You deserve any man to spend some of his bag on you."

"Well, still in all, I'm thankful." She smiled and kissed my cheek. "I can tell that there is something wrong with you. Do you care to share with me?"

I shook my head. "Not really, it's just trap shit." I gripped her big booty and kept it clenched.

She nodded. "Still in all, I wanna know what's going on with my man. I don't like you being so closed off with me." She rubbed the side of my face. "Can we sit down and talk for a minute?"

I sighed and took a hold of her hand. "Yeah, come on." I guided her through the dimly lit club and headed to the back where our table was. We took a seat and ordered our food.

Tasia leaned across the table and took hold of two of my fingers. "Well, baby, talk to me. What's going on inside that big head of yours?" She laughed.

"On some real shit?"

"Yeah, be honest with me." She placed her smaller hand inside mine. "Please."

"Yo', even though it's been two weeks. I still can't get my mind off my sister. She ain't returning none of my calls, and my mother says she ain't been home in the same length of time. I keep trying to wrap my head around how she got to the place that she's in. I didn't see it coming. She has always been so precious to me."

"Aww baby, I'm sure she's okay. Hermes has always been strong. Right now, she's fighting a demon, and if we know anything about Hermes she likes to do things alone. She feels like it makes her stronger that way."

"Yeah, but she ain't alone. I love my sister, and I would do anything for her with no hesitation."

"I know you would." Tasia rubbed the top of my hand and smiled warmly. "I know you're hurting, right now but I need you to know that I love you and that I'm here for you, always. Do you know that?"

I looked across the table at her. "You already know it's really hard for me to trust anybody. So, I ain't gon' blow smoke up ya' ass and make it seem like everything is peachy keen. Honestly, when it comes to us, I don't even know where we stand. We haven't really discussed that."

Tasia took her hand back and gave me a crazy look. "Damn, what made you say something like that?"

"Just trying to keep us as close to reality as we can be. And the reality is that every single day I'm getting blindsided with somethin' new. If it ain't something from the family, then, it's something from the Trenches. I feel like I ain't even in a position to be loved or to love. My life could end any day, and then what? You can't do shit then but find another nigga to take my place and fill my shoes. You'll probably forget about me in less than a month." I sat back and poured myself some of the wine, drank half the glass, and poured myself some more about the same amount.

"Damn, it's crazy to see how you really look at me. This whole time, I thought that you and I were together. Come to find out that you have it in your mind that we are just what? Friends or something. Friends that don't trust each other?" She sat back and crossed her arms.

"Yo', I ain't saying that. All I'm saying is that we never established our position in each other's lives. So, we been rocking from day to day with no clarity." I didn't know why I was lashing out at her, but I couldn't help it. I was hurting over the state of Hermes and Tasia was the closest person to me for me to give the business to, so I seized the opportunity to do so.

She cleared her throat. "You know what, Tyson, how about we start by doing this? What do you need from me?"

I shrugged my shoulders. "I don't know. Other than pussy, I really ain't seeing nothing I would need, even then yo' pussy ain't really a need, it's more of a convenient want."

The waiter came and placed our plates in front of us. She fit napkins into our laps and bowed her dreadlocked head before she walked away from the table. I caught a glimpse of her ass and saw that it was fat.

"No, you didn't just say that the only worth I had to me was my pussy. I know you've been holding me down, but you got me all the way fucked up. You're basically saying I'm worthless to you."

"N'all, that's what you're saying. You asked me what I needed from you and I told you."

"So, why did you save me then, Tyson, huh? What made you risk your life to save a person that the most you see in them is what they have between their thighs? That's what I don't get. Why would you get into all that drama with both King, and Kammron over me if the only thing you see in me is the gap between my legs?"

Because me saving you doesn't have anything to do with sex. I stepped into your situation because I wasn't with dude hurting you in the fashion that he was. No female should ever have to go through what you did, and the fact that Kammron would take advantage of a little girl that he helped raise is sick to me. I can't understand that nigga, and I don't want to. But with all that said, I honestly care about you. I have cared about you for a long time."

"You sho' got a funny way of showing it." She rolled her eyes and laughed. "Do you wanna be with me? Like, can you see me as your girl for a long time?"

"I don't even see me being alive for a long time." I looked off. "I already know that my days are numbered. I got way too many niggas at my head. Sooner or later, somebody gon' catch me slipping, and that's gon' be that."

"Don't say that, Tyson. Why would you speak that into existence? You don't know your future. You gotta leave that up to God."

"N'all, I know mine, and I already know that before I hit twenty-five, it's gon' be a wrap for me. But that's cool because until then, I'm finna' cause hell all over the city of New York. I ain't one hunnit percent certain on how. But when I figure it out mafuckas gon' be in trouble." I took a sip of my iced tea and looked across the table at her.

She lowered her head. "Oh, well, I hope you don't die all early and stuff. I like the man that you are and I gotta say that you are the first man that I know has pure intentions with me. Only thing about that is, I don't know if I'm even worthy to be loved by you. I've been through so much in my life, and Kammron says that I'm not anything more than damaged goods. I don't really know what that means, but I can guess." She shook her head, and it appeared that her face got closer to her lap.

"Tasia, don't ever put no weight into what that fool, Kammron said. Any man that can help raise a little girl, and years later wind up going in on her like she's the average female on the street, trying to force himself on her, fuckin' her and all that, ain't even a man. That nigga is a bitch. Word to Brooklyn, I wish I would've smoked that punk. I think the reason it's so hard for me to look at you in a sexual manner is because of everything that you've been through. All I wanna do is care for you and treat you like my sister. Lord knows I wish I could have done so many things differently with her."

"Your sister, Tyson, really? Damn, so you don't look at me as your woman at all? Wow!" She sat back and crossed her arms. "I don't even know what to take from that. I guess on the one hand I should feel secure in what we have as friends, but on the other hand, it's like I really do like you as a man. I wanna be with you. Ever since you and I have met, I've always known that I was going to be your girl. Things were so cool before you went to Jamaica. Then when you came back, all of a sudden you were married, I was devastated. I saw the little fantasy of you and I being together slipping out of the window. I hated it, especially after seeing what your new wife looked like. I already knew there was no way I could compete with her. How you've somehow chosen me over her is still mind-boggling to me. But now I get it. You're choosing me as a sister, and not as a woman." She swallowed her spit and appeared choked up.

"Tasia, stop looking at what I said and finding ways to pick it apart to make our situation worse." I sipped from my tea again. "I'm not fit to be nobody's man, right now. I got way too much shit going on in life to be trying to settle down with a woman. Every day that you and I are together, I am putting your life in danger, and that ain't cool."

"But I wouldn't even have a life if you didn't save it. I don't care about the dangers I face in being with you. The fact of the matter is that I love you, Tyson, and I want you to love me, too. Is that so hard for you to do?" She hugged herself and bounced her feet on her toes almost nervously.

I was silent for a long time because I really didn't know what to say to her. Even though I cared about Tasia I couldn't get the thought out of my mind that she had come from such a broken past. I didn't know how to go about being with her. I was a very sexual person, and with my woman, that's how I wanted to always be. But when I thought about coming at her like that, I couldn't help but feel like whatever I did would make her think about me in terms of Kammron so I always caught myself.

"I don't even know why you brought me out here now. I feel so stupid." She began to pick over her food.

"Damn, Tasia, I do like you and all that shit, but I just don't know how to handle or be with you. Every time I look at that fat ass booty, I wanna squeeze that mafucka' every time

I watch you walk, I think about what that pussy will be like, and every time you hug me, I want to snatch you up. That shit doesn't make me no different than Kammron because all I am doing is sexualizing you."

"Yeah, but that's okay, Tyson because you aren't my father, or whatever. You're my boyfriend. You're supposed to think about me in those terms, and it's okay." She reached across the table and took a hold of my hand. "Is that why you and I haven't been together ever since you found out about Kammron?"

Before I could answer her question, my father, King, came into the restaurant with a group of Jamaican head bussahs. He walked to the front of the restaurant where all patrons were supposed to check in to be given a table. I was sure that he hadn't seen me. Then, Ashlynn came through the doors sporting a quarter length, coca-cola mink. She and I locked eyes, and she made her way over to the table.

T.J. Edwards

Chapter 7

"Wow, so you mean to tell me that while I'm sitting here seven months pregnant. You're out fuckin' off on me with this bitch? Ugh, I should have known." She turned up her nose and mugged Tasia.

Tasia looked across the table at me, then up at her with a slight smile on her face. "Why the fuck would he care about you being pregnant? Or would he be anywhere near your trifling ass, when nine times out of ten, the baby you're carrying is his father's?" She sipped from her tea.

Ashlynn glared her hazel eyes into Tasia's brown ones. "No, you didn't just say that. Somebody needs to muzzle this bitch." She pulled a blade out of her waistband so fast that it caught me off guard. She slammed the handle of it on the table. "And I would love to be the one that stopped you from talking permanently."

Tasia placed her purse on the table and snuck her hand into it. "Good thing I'm licensed to carry a concealed weapon. Give me the rights to knock a stupid bitch's head off, permanently." She lowered her eyes.

Ashlynn started to shake, still eyeing her with hatred. She looked around the restaurant and began nodding her head. "Yeah, okay, Tasia. I got you. I'ma let you get off right now, but I got yo' ass."

"Bitch, I'll be waiting." Tasia sat her purse in her lap and kept her hand inside it. I didn't know if she really had a pistol in there or not, but she sure kept her hand ducked deep as if she really did.

Ashlynn turned to me. "So, when are you coming home? I miss you."

"Shorty, you really wanna do this here, huh?" I started feeling myself and getting heated.

I was also wondering why my father hadn't made his way over here to say something to me? He'd already looked over and spotted me twice. I could only imagine that it meant he was over me coming home, and I had two strikes left before he found a way to take my life.

"Yes, I really do wanna do this here, because you need to give me a fuckin' answer. I am your wife, and you aren't telling me anything. It's been nearly seven months. What the fuck is your problem?"

I hopped up. "Bitch, did you forget you was fucking my Pops? Did you forget I told yo' ass and him, that I didn't give a fuck about Jamaica, and I don't give a fuck about you? As far as I'm concerned, you two muthafuckas can have each other. I'm over that shit. Any more questions?"

"You damn right I have some more questions. What if this doesn't turn out to be King's baby, and it's yours. Then what?" She stepped into my face.

Tasia hopped up. "You don't need to be all in his face like that. He can hear you from over there," she said pointing to where Ashlynn was standing previously.

"Tasia, shut up, this doesn't concern you," Ashlynn said without taking her eyes off me.

"Yo, if that's my seed, I'ma be stomp down and make sure it's straight. I ain't never been no fuck nigga, but at the same time, I don't want shit to do with you, or that black ass nigga over there." I nodded my head at King.

"Yeah, I already know that, and it's understandable. But what isn't, is what are you going to do if they kill you for treason against the Fast Money Cartel, against Jamrock? You are supposed to be the prince? How are you missing this?"

"Shorty, if they kill me, they kill me. But, I ain't bowing down to no nigga and accepting no bitch that I can't trust. I don't fear death, and I don't fear, King. It ain't shit he can do to me that I can't do to him. If any nigga thinks I'ma live my life enslaved to him, obviously he don't know who I am, nor what I am willing to die for." I lowered my eyes and leaned closer to her face. "I don't want shit to do with you, Ashlynn. In my opinion, you ain't nothing but a sneaky, low life, Jamaican bitch that plays both sides. I wouldn't be surprised if you really had something to do with Manifest being killed. That shit seems like it's in your nature."

Her eyes were low at first, and then they opened widely. "No, the fuck you didn't just say some shit like that to me." She balled up her fists.

"I said what I meant, and that's just that. Come on, Tasia, baby, let's get up out of here." I pulled out a few hundred dollars and placed it inside our bill collector for the table. Then I held out my hand for Tasia to take.

Tasia took my hand and gave Ashlynn a smirk. "Well, sister girl, I do wish you the best. Sorry that things didn't work out in your favor, or do I mean not sorry?" She looked serious. "Bitch, you do the math."

Ashlynn nodded her head over and over. "Okay, Tyson. I see what this is. I got you, though. I got you and this bitch. Y'all gon' on and enjoy your short lives. Long live, King Locust, and long live Jamrock. It's official." She turned her back and walked off mumbling under her breath.

Tasia smiled bright and rushed to place her arms around my neck. "Damn, that shit just got me so hot and bothered. You did dat, Tyson."

***

When we got home, Tasia wasn't playing any games. As soon as we walked through the threshold of the door frame, she dropped to her knees and went for the buckle of my pants.

She opened them, and my belt so fast, I didn't even know they were down until I felt her pulling my boxers down next. Then she had my piece in her hand stroking it up and down. "I want you so bad, Tyson. I can't believe we've been together this long, and we ain't never went this far at least."

I knew I was long overdue. I placed my hand on top of her head and allowed her to do what she was getting ready to do. "Yo', forget all that, Shorty, gon' head and bless me."

"You think I ain't?" She pulled downward and sucked the head into her mouth. "Mmm." She popped it back out and licked around it before sucking it again. "Mmm. Mmm. Mmm."

My hips began moving, trying to get her to take more into her mouth. "Bless me, Shorty, stop playing. Where is Brooklyn at?"

Saying this made her suck me faster and take me deeper into her throat. Her sucking noises got louder and louder. She danced with her lips all over me. It kept feeling better and better. I groaned and tightened my grip on her hair. This made her start deep throating me as best she could.

"Suck that dick, baby! Suck that dick. Damn, I'm finna' fuck the shit out of yo' lil' thick ass."

She smiled, closed her eyes, and started sucking faster. Spit dripped from her bottom lip. She popped me out and pumped me at full speed. "I wanna taste you so bad. All I wanna do is taste you, Tyson. Please cum in my mouth. Please." She sucked me back in and started sucking so hard, and fast that I stood on my tiptoes and started breathing hard. Her lips were so juicy, and it felt so good. She squeezed me in her small hand, and it was too much.

"Aww fuck, boo, I'm cumming." I grabbed her hair tighter and started fucking her mouth. Long stroking her face while I jerked, and came back-to-back, shivering.

Tasia choked but kept swallowing. Her jaws hollowed in and out, and then she pulled back and pumped me slowly causing cum to seep out of the top of my piece. Her tongue swiped it away. "I want you now, Tyson. Please, I feel like I've been wanting you for an eternity."

I backed up and picked her up. I had to space my feet just a little bit because Tasia had a bit of weight on her. She was what we liked to call in Brooklyn, slim-thick. Once I had her picked up, we locked lips. I kissed all over hers and licked along the side of her neck before I bit into it. My teeth pulled hungrily at her jugular.

"Uunnnhhh, Tyson. I want you so bad, baby. I swear to God, I do." She threw her head back and moaned at the top of her lungs.

I carried her to the bed and laid her back on it. I pulled the dress up just enough so that it sat on top of her small, early B cup titties. Her nipples were so hard that they were sticking up through the material of the Victoria Secrets bra that she had over them. I sucked the buds through the material.

She arched her back. "Unnhhh fuck, I need you so bad, Tyson. Please take me, I don't care about shit but you."

I opened the bra and her breasts fell out into my gaze. I cupped them. "Yo', I been fiending for you, too, cutie. I just ain't know how to go about dis' part." I sucked her left nipple into my mouth and pulled it before switching to the right one.

"Just regular, baby. I ain't no different. Please just treat me regularly." She arched her back and delivered herself to me.

I kissed all over her breasts and took my time sucking her nipples until they were so long that they stood up like pencil erasers. "I gotta have this body. I gotta have you, Tasia." I pulled her dress all the way off and slid her panties to the side.

My fingers found her gap. Her pussy lips were puffed out on each side. They looked fully engorged and a reddish-brown. I stuck my nose down there and sniffed her box, just like her mother had taught me to do when she showed me how to eat pussy. I needed to make sure Tasia was fresh down there before I did what I wanted to do to her. One whiff told me that she was fresh as a summer breeze. I pulled the panties further to the side and stuck my nose directly into the center of her lips and sniffed hard.

She opened her thick thighs wider. "Ooohhh, fuck, Tyson." Her feet came up until they lined up with her shoulder blades. She had that thang bussed wide open.

I fixed the crotch of the panties so that they separated her lips, then I sucked on the flesh of her sex just like that. I got sloppy, yet, precise with it and started making so much noise from my munching that she started going crazy, and my penis got harder and harder.

"I'm 'bout to make you cum, Shorty. Watch, I'm 'bout to make this fat ass pussy come, right now." I pulled her pussy lips all the way back and trapped her clitoris. I sucked and flicked my tongue over it again and again. Then I made circles around it, before sucking lightly. Two fingers slipped inside her hole, and I ran them out at full speed.

"Unh! Unh! Unh!" She bucked into my face and laid her face sideways on the mattress. "I swear to God! Uhhhh! I swear to God! I love you! I love you! I love youuu! Uh, fuck!" She sat all the way up and forced my face further into her gap.

I licked from side to side, up and down, and sucked her clit into my lips as if it were a piece of Oyster. Her juices flowed down my lips and dripped off my chin. It was so hard I couldn't help pumping my piece while she came all over my tongue, nose, and lips. When she was done, I sat back on my legs and rubbed her gap from side to side as fast as I could.

She held her thighs wide open with her eyes closed. Her juices were in her crease. "Ooohhh, Tyson. Come on now, baby. Fuck me. It's been long enough." She sat up and pulled me down on top of her.

I got up. "Shorty, you ain't runnin' shit. I got this." I slipped from the bed and pulled her to the edge. Once there, I flipped her over and brought her up to all fours. I took my hand and rubbed over those chubby cheeks that were just perfect for me. Her ass was fat.

She spaced her knees and looked back over her shoulder at me. "I'm yours, Tyson. I don't give a fuck what goes on in life. I belong to you. I'm your bitch." She laid her face on the bed and spaced her knees a bit more.

"Yo', I already know that. That's why I got you forever, cutie." I smacked that ass and rubbed over it.

My boxers were already on the floor. I took the head of my dick, eased it past her puffy sex lips and into her heat. The deeper I got it felt like the tighter she became. I gripped her hips on the side and pushed harder.

"Unnnhhh, Tyson, baby, fuck." She looked back at me and pushed backward.

I dug my fingers into her hips and pulled her all the way back until I was nine plus inches deep. I spaced my feet again and went to work, long stroking that pussy, just like I'd done when I fucked her mother. "Gimme dis shit. Gimme dis pussy, Tasia."

"Uh! Uh! Uh! It's yours! It's yours, baby." She kept her face on the bed and pushed back over and over again, harder and harder, taking my dick like a champion.

Smack! Smack! Smack! Smack!

I slapped that ass over and over again. It seemed like every time I did, she got wetter. "Fuck that other shit call me Daddy. I'm Daddy now!" *Smack!* "Say it!" I slapped that ass hard.

"Uhhhh shit!" She came and started shaking so bad that at first, I thought something was wrong. Her juices leaked off my balls, and down my thighs. "Daddy! Uhhhh, Daddy! I love you, Tyson."

"You my bitch. I got you! I got you, Shorty!" I clenched my teeth and stroked her as hard as I could, and as fast as I could before I felt that familiar feeling. My whole body began to tingle.

She placed her palms on the bed, and looked back at me, milking my dick. "Uh! Uh! Uh! Uhhhh! I'm cumming, Daddy! I'm cumming!" She tilted her head toward the ceiling and screamed at the top of her lungs.

I slammed into her over and over. As soon as I felt like I was about to cum, I pulled out and bussed all over her pretty ass big booty. I mean it came out in jets. I kept looking down at how her pussy lips were slightly opened, and it drove me crazy? One thing for sure was that Tasia had some good ass pussy just like her mother.

Chapter 8

Bomp! Bomp! Bomp! Bomp!

By the time I jumped out of bed and made it downstairs to see who it was. I had two pistols in my hands, and Maze was beating on the door again. I opened it and he walked straight in talking a mile a minute. I couldn't understand shit he was saying and trying to start to get on my nerves.

"Yo', calm ya' ass down and tell me what's good." I closed the door to my crib and locked it.

"Niggas got me fucked up, B. I just got stripped, and two of my traps just got ran in. I recognized one of them niggas, and he definitely works for, Bonkers. Yo', I feel like the kid was targeted." Maze, paced back and forth with his face balled up."

"So, what are you saying? You tryna' holla at blood 'nem, right now. Let me get dressed and I'm wit' you." I made my way toward the back of the house.

"Yo', you do that. I'm tryna tear some shit up real quick before mafuckas even wake up all the way. I've been in Red Hook all my life and ain't nobody ever tried me like they did last night. Yo', I feel like a fuckin' goofy. Word to the Borough." He lowered his head and punched his hand.

"Nigga, pick ya' head up. Getting stripped is part of the game. At least you got away from that bitch with your life. We gon' clap at them niggas and see what it do. Give me a minute, I'ma be ready to roll." I left him standing there nodding his head.

When I got to the back room Tasia was laid on her stomach with the covers only over her waist on down. That big booty caused the sheets to form a wedgie, and it looked so good. I couldn't take my eyes off it. I sat on the bed, and kissed that ass, before biting it softly.

"Mmm, Daddy." She opened her eyes and looked back at me. "There you go already. Dang, you ain't get enough of me last night?"

"Hell n'all I didn't. If I did, do you think I would still be all up in ya ass like this?" I stuffed my face into the crux between her thighs and sniffed hard. It smelled like straight pussy, a clean version, though.

She came to her knees and pulled the covers down. Her meaty crease came into view. I played with the sex lips, squeezing them together. They felt so good to me. She smiled and licked the lips on her face.

"Well, at least I know you like my body. That makes me feel really good." She turned all the way around and stood up until she and I were face to face. "Yo', I don't wanna kill the moment or nothing, but I been telling you that I love you every day and you ain't said that shit once? What's the deal?"

I grabbed her closer to me and kissed her lips. I sucked them and slipped my tongue into her mouth. "One thing for sure, I don't be kissing bitches that I don't care about. Secondly, I wouldn't allow no woman to sleep beside me in my bed, while my defenses are down if I didn't feel a way about her. Thirdly, everything don't need a label, and you can't always identify a thug's feelings."

She raised her left eyebrow. "So, do you love me or not? I'm confused."

I laughed. "I'ma hold you down with my life. I'll never forsake, nor allow anybody to hurt you. I feel like you are under my domain and it's my job to be there for you. But as far as love goes, my heart's too black for that. I don't love anybody but my mother and sister."

She dropped her head. "Ain't nobody ever loved me for me. Especially not any men. I don't know what it is about me that makes a man stop short of that." She sighed.

I tilted her chin up and looked into her pretty, brown eyes. "Hey, Shorty, why don't you quit worrying about how these nothing ass niggas feel about you, and love yourself? If you would simply love you, then you wouldn't give a fuck how another nigga feels about you. That's the real."

"Yeah, I know, but I'm a woman. I'm more emotional than you are. Plus, I really like you, and it would mean the world to me if you like me too enough to love me." She shook her head. "If you don't love me. Who's to say that one of these days you won't kick me to the curb for another woman? Then what would I have?"

"Yourself, and because you are a woman, and you have yourself, you are stronger than you think. Never forget that. My mother is the strongest human being I have ever met in my entire life. I don't get my strength from my father, King. I get my strength from her and that makes me proud to be able to say that. Before I finish, I would never kick you to the curb, or replace you with some other woman. You and I are jammed tight. I got your back as long as you show me your loyalty and love."

"Well, that makes me feel good." She exhaled loudly. "I think I have to just get up and get my own. That way I won't be so dependent on you and I won't spend every moment when you and I aren't together worrying if you're going to bring somebody home that is better than me, just to kick me to the curb. That's the part that scares me."

I held her small face in my hands. "Baby, we ain't in high school no more. I ain't some immature lil' dude that's trying to bag every female that comes across my path. n'all, I'm something like a major nigga. I got money, and I got plans to get richer. I can't trust just any bitch around me. The only reason you are able to sleep in this bed beside me every night is because I trust you, and I see you as my baby. Fuck love, that means more to me than love. Come here." I guided her until she was kissing my lips.

She smiled. "Yeah, Daddy. Well, even though all that makes sense, I still love you and I'm gon' fight for you until you love me just the same."

Maze came and stuck his face into the room. "Blood, what the fuck? Nigga, I need yo' ass now, and you up in here on this lovey-dovey ass shit. Let's go, now! I'm ready to kill some niggas." He slapped the side of the door and left the room.

I mugged where he once stood until I calmed down. "Yo', kid wilding."

Tasia grabbed me close and kissed my lips. "I love you and be careful. I'm gon' clean up this house from top to bottom, then cook for you. Be safe, Daddy, I'll be here when you get back."

I kissed her again. "That's all I need to hear. Later, baby.

***

"Yo', kid bitch got you wilding, Tyson, word up. You ain't never had a nigga waiting like that when it came to bidness. Usually, you be on yo' game, Dunn. That's why I don't like her lil' irritating ass." Maze was mugging the side of my head? He'd already downed half a Sprite bottle of Lean with two Purks inside it.

I kept loading my F&N. "Bruh, I don't know what you're talking about. Me and Shorty were only talking for a minute, maybe two, before you brought yo' lil' rude ass up there to break some shit up. We had a moment. I needed that shit, too, so be smooth. Everything ain't always gotta be hardcore, you know?"

"Yo', please don't tell me you're falling for this bitch? Please tell me you're just living in the moment." He looked over at me.

"Nigga, don't worry about my love life. Long as you on top of ya own shit, you should be alright."

"Aw, come on, Tyson. You already know how this shit goes out in the field. We ain't got room to be loving no bitch, B. Our days are numbered. Plus, we need to be getting our connects in order so we can take over Brooklyn. Once we flat line that nigga Bonkers the borough is for the taking."

"Fuck that gotta do wit' me and Tasia?"

Maze shook his head. "So, now it actually is you and Tasia? Really, Kid?" He sighed. "Yo', when it comes to this game, bruh, you can lose a whole lot of money chasing bitches, but you'll never lose one bitch chasing money. You gain them. They come by the thousands. I just don't think it's wise, this early in the game to be chasing shorty. She needs to fall back, and you gotta get yo' money right. Especially if you're trying to lead this whole thang. Ain't I been doing my part by letting you lead, even though you got in the field way after me?"

I nodded. "I ain't think that far into things. I just thought we was getting money together. For me, it ain't always gotta be a lead or follow type thing. I say let's get it together."

"N'all, B, that's not how the game works. Somebody gotta be the head. You got the connects, so I let you lead. I just make sure the troops and the guns stay cocked and loaded. I'm cool wit' that part, word up." He snickered. "How the fuck you gon' wife a bitch that been ran through anyway? This is Brooklyn, son, it's plenty of young hoes in the borough that ain't got as many miles on them as Tasia do. You are a Don or at least you're on your way to being one. If you gon' snatch up a bitch, she gotta be bad and she gotta be a bitch that ain't, too many niggas can say they hit. After all that shit that went on with Kammron and those Flatbush niggas. I don't know if we can say for certain that Tasia is worthy to be seated beside a king in the making. I mean that's just my opinion."

"You're right, Blood, that is just your opinion. And do you think I give a real fuck about how you feeling or thinking? Huh, nigga? Do I pick apart the hoes you call yourself laying down with? Most of those bitches be rough as hell, by the way, but I ain't fuckin' them, so it ain't my bidness."

"Yo', you just not getting what I'm saying, that's all. If you knew how to look at shit, you wouldn't be so offended."

"Offended? Boi, you ain't said shit to offend me. I'm secure in me. I'm fucking wit' shorty, that's just that. You can keep yo' opinions to yourself."

"Yeah, alright, Tyson. You gon' head and fuck wit' shorty then. All I wanna know is what the fuck are you going to do if we gotta blow her mom's down, huh?"

I shrugged my shoulders. "If that's something we gotta do, then I guess we'll cross that bridge when we come to it. Until then, we move how we move. I don't wanna hear shit else about my love life, especially if I ain't commenting on your shit? Alright'?"

"Shit, fuck you then. I'll keep my comments to myself." He stepped on the gas and kept a mug on his face.

I didn't care, I didn't like nobody in my business. Even though me and the homey cool it was imperative that he stayed in his lane. If it was one way to lose me as a friend, being all up in my business was one of the ways to have me sever ties with you immediately. Shit like that reminded me of being under King's thumb for nearly nineteen straight years. Now that I was no longer under it, I avoided the feeling of being trapped by anybody one hundred percent.

***

I waited until Maze, got beside the door ready to run inside, before I cocked back my foot, and kicked as hard as I could. *Whoom!* The door flew inward, I stepped to the side. Maze zipped past me and ran inside the broken door with two guns in his hand. I upped my guns and ran in behind him. From right to left, everywhere I looked, I saw three dope boys and two females trying to run for cover. Maze wasn't having it. I also saw a bunch of money and dope all over a rounded wooden table.

"You mafuckas got the nerve to try and rob the god!"

Blocka! Blocka! Blocka! Blocka! His gun spit one round after the next, bodies dropped.

I watched bullets tear up backs before they fell to the floor with a look of pain spread across their faces. Maze stepped over them and sent two more slugs into the back of the two dope boy's heads before he went chasing the last one, bussing at him. He hit him twice in the back knocking him into the wall, where he slid down it in slow motion.

The two females took off running in the opposite direction toward me. Maze stopped in his tracks and turned around. He aimed at them and allowed his gun to go off back-to-back. *Blocka! Blocka! Blocka!* One female fell right by my feet. She twisted and laid on her side. Maze hopped over her and shot her friend four times before he turned back around and finished the first female with two shots.

He looked up at me. "That's what I think about a bitch, bruh. Fuck these hoes. Come on. Look at all my money and dope all over that mafuckin' table. Let's get it and bounce."

That's exactly what we did, then we hit it out the back door, ran down the steps, and hopped in the stolen Buick that we kept running. Maze breathed hard for the first ten blocks with an evil smile on his face.

"I love that killing shit, Boss. Man, that shit just does somethin' to me." He stepped on the gas and sped onto the highway then he started going the regular speed limit.

Chapter 9

"Tyson, you don't think your mother is going to have a fit with you bringing me over here with you? The way she sounded on the phone was like she was excited to finally spend some time with her son all alone. I think she's about to give you the business," Tasia said, acting like she was timid to hold my hand as we stepped up on my mother's stoop.

"Shorty, I know my mother. She's a very straightforward person, and like I said, she is one of the strongest people I have ever met in my entire life. If she's feeling some type of way, she will let us know right away, but she won't be rude about it."

"And if that's the case then what do I do?" Tasia looked up at me nervously.

"You don't do anything, we will just bounce and I'll find another time to come over and meet her. I simply chose today at this time, solely because King is out of the country on business."

"I figured as much." She took a deep breath and looked up at the two-story house. "Well, she and I haven't ever had many words. I don't know why I feel so damn nervous. Maybe it's because I know how much she really means to you and I just want her to like me." She turned to me. "If she doesn't, will you hate me?"

I laughed. "Shorty, you're good. Just be yourself, and let's go in here and enjoy my moms', she good people." I stepped forward and was about to ring the doorbell when the door opened.

"I've been sitting here for two minutes wondering when either one of you was going to ring the bell. All you've been doing is whispering all secretively. Come on inside. Did you come to see me or to have a secret meeting on my stoop?" She looked back and forth from me to Tasia.

I wasn't trying to hear that. I stepped forward, pulled her into my arms, and picked her up, spinning her around on the porch. "Yo', I been missing you like crazy, mama. How have you been?" I placed her back on her small feet. She'd turned a beet red. She slapped my shoulder. "Boy, what did I tell you about taking me off my feet? You are my son. Such feelings shouldn't be felt by me for you." She closed her eyes and hugged my neck.

I kissed both of her cheeks, then her forehead. "Whatever, I been picking you up ever since I was twelve years old, and I'ma keep doing it. You're my beautiful mother and ain't nothing you can do about it." I smiled and took a step back. "Mama, this is my girlfriend, Tasia. I know you already know who she is, but I wanted to formally reintroduce you two. Tasia, this is the love of my life, and the strongest person I know.

My mother, Janelle moved me to the side and extended her hand to Tasia. "So, you're the gal that has been holding my son down? Are you troubled, or are you more submissive to him?"

Tasia's eyes got bucked. She looked over at me. "Uh, I would like to say that I am submissive. I don't give him a hard time, and I allow him to come and go as he pleases."

My mother clicked her tongue against her teeth. "A submissive woman can be both a blessing and a curse. In order for a household to flourish, the woman must follow her intuitions. She must be both submissive and assertive. You can never allow a man to come and go as he pleases. He will always go more than come with that type of leeway. God created balances for everything in life, and the scale is always supposed to be straight down the middle. Even. Come on in, Ms. Girlfriend." She smiled and finished shaking her hand.

As soon as we stepped into the house, that strong scent of Caribbean food came rushing toward me. It smelled so good that my stomach began to growl almost immediately. I lowered my eyes, and a smile came across my face. "Yo', mama, that's the scent I been missing right there. Dang, you always got a way of making me feel so homesick."

"That's my job. Why have you been away for so long? Do you not know that your mother misses you more and more each day?" She guided us to the kitchen table where we were directed to take a seat.

The kitchen was clean and organized. Everything was top of the line and with a Caribbean effect. Several dishes aligned the table covered with aluminum foil.

"The last thing I need is to run into Pops, right now. I don't know how he feels, or what's going on with him," I said, pulling out Tasia's chair and waiting for her to take a seat, then pushing it in for her.

"Thank you, baby," Tasia, uttered softly.

"Of course, boo." I rushed around to do the same for my mother's chair.

She looked me over suspiciously. "Wow, you get her chair before you even get my own. She must really be special to you." She took a seat and allowed me to push her closer to the table.

Once seated, she began taking the aluminum foil off the dishes, uncovering some of the most gorgeous food I'd seen in all my life. My stomach growled again.

"Stop that, Goddess. Nobody comes before you. You are my life, but yes, this is my baby right here," I let it be known. Tasia smiled at me.

"Does she know that you are technically married?" My mother asked without looking up at me. She dumped curried chicken on to her plate and handed the bowl to Tasia.

"Mama, come on now," I started.

"Yes, ma'am, I know about Ashlynn and their arranged marriage. Tyson rarely keeps anything from me," Tasia let it be known. She dumped some of the chicken on her plate.

"And you are still willing to be his mistress knowing that he is in a full marriage? One that may result in death, might I add." She eyed her closely.

"I am willing to die for Tyson. He is the love of my life, and I accept him and his situations for what they are. I will stand by him until my last breath," Tasia promised.

My mother laughed. "Those are strong words coming from such a young girl. You two barely know each other. Ashlynn has been plotting and begging for permission to take your life. Once King gives it to her, I feel sorry for your well being. Knowing this, are you still ready to die to be with him?"

Tasia nodded. "I sure am. I love him, and when it comes to this life, there is nobody that I am willing to stand by more than him, and that's even in the shadow of danger. He's always had my back, and therefore I will always have his."

My mother handed her the rice. "How much do you value your life, little gal?" She raised her right eyebrow.

Tasia placed rice on my plate first, then added some to her own. "I mean I don't know. Ever since I've been alive, life hasn't been so friendly to me. The only ray of sunshine that I have comes from your son. He, for me, makes this painful life worth living."

"Aww, isn't that stupid?" My mother rolled her eyes at her. "You are a child. You know nothing about sacrificing your life for a man or being ready and willing to die for him. Thinking the way you're thinking will only get you two places. One, you'll be in the grave faster than you can think, or two, you will wind up in a broken, loveless marriage with a man that takes you for granted. As a woman, you should always strive to put yourself and your needs first. Once they are established and taken care of, then, and only then, will you be able to be what you need to be for him, but not until then." She loaded up her plate with the rest of the fixings that were around the table. "So, tell me, Tasia, how old are you?"

"Mama, why are you doing this?" I asked, getting slightly angry with her third degree.

"Tyson, when I am ready to speak to you, I will call your name. Until then, shut up. Tasia, answer the question."

Tasia looked over at me and I nodded my head for her to answer my mother's question. Tasia cleared her throat. "I'll be twenty in March."

"So, it is as I've said, you are a baby." My mother smiled and began to buss down her chicken.

"With all due respect, Janelle, I don't need to be fifty years old to know that I love your son. I don't need gray hair to be growing out of my head to know that this man is who I am ready and willing to be faithful to and crazy about. I am a one-man woman, and I want and need to be that for him. I do not fear the things that he is wrapped up in. If anything happens to him, then let it happen to me as well. I am not concerned about his past because I am undoubtedly his future. So, bring with them what they may, and we will face them together. Any more questions?" She waited for a moment and started to eat her food.

My mother kept silent for a moment. Then she started to smile, and I knew she was about to get on bullshit. "All the things you've said sounds very good. Any mother would love for a son to bring home a woman, and she speaks exactly the way that you have. But there is only one thing bothering me, right now. Do you want to know what that is?"

Tasia dropped her fork and rested her thumb and forefinger along the side of her face. "You know what, Janelle, please enlighten me."

My mother smiled as if she was up to something again. "The whole time you've been talking Tyson has not stepped in to say how he feels for you. You have gone to the extreme with your statements, and not once has he backed your feelings with those of his own. Why is that, Tyson?"

"Yo', moms, why are you doing this, right now, huh? I thought you called me over so I could spend some time with you and enjoy this delicious meal that my Queen put together for me. Why do you gotta ruin it with all of this prying?" I wanted to know.

She wagged her finger from side to side. "Uh-uh, you're not about to get off that easy. I wanna know how you really feel about this girl? So, tell me? She says that she is willing to die for you and stand beside you no matter what the consequences are. She says that she is willing to accept any fate, pretty much, as long as she is beside you. Are you willing to do the same?"

I sighed and lowered my head. "Yo', this is real foul, right now. I ain't come over here to discuss me and her relationship. I came over here to see and be with you. I wanted to reintroduce you two and enjoy spending some time with you. That's it, and that's all."

My mother smiled harder. "I figured that would be your response, and that is all I need to know. Tasia, you need to protect yourself and your heart. Your feelings are way too strong, and I am telling you as a woman first, and as his mother secondly, that you are way ahead of him emotionally. You're so high up, that whenever he does what all men do, you'll have so far to fall that you won't be able to recover. That is dangerous." She began eating her food again. "I like you, I think you are beautiful and strong. But I also think you are emotionally dumb. That is dangerous."

"Wow, Ms. Janelle, you sure don't hold any punches do you?" Tasia asked, pushing her plate from in front of her. She looked sick.

"It's not in my nature to do so. I am who I am. I have allowed myself to be broken beyond repair a long time ago. Little girl, I was you. I might not be able to tell you your beginning, but I can tell you your middle, and your ending. Both are grim." My mother started eating her food as if suddenly a weight had been lifted off her shoulders. "Oh, kids, enjoy." She beamed.

***

An hour later, we were sitting in the living room with me holding my mother's hands, knee to knee, looking into her eyes. I took a deep breath and tried to listen to the things that she was telling me while I tried my best to push the way she'd acted toward Tasia out of my mind. I felt angered, disrespected, and offended by all of it. But this was still my mother, and I chose her.

"Son, as you know, ever since me and your father have come to be, I have always hated his roots and the island of Jamaica. They treated me so horribly in the past. They did things to me that I will never forgive, and until my last breath I will always feel an utter disdain within myself for that entire situation." She took a deep breath, and slowly breathed it out.

"However, there comes a time in a woman's life when she has to make some scary decisions for the greater good of her family, and the future. For me, this is one of those times." She swallowed and continued, "Baby, things are about to get entirely serious between you and your father. He is less than a month away from giving the go-ahead on your life. So, it is imperative that you prepare for the unknown, and that you surround yourself with as much security detail as possible. In order to do this, you will need a substantial amount of money, guns, and product to flood the streets. You need to feed as many starving, low-life degenerates as you can so that they will pledge their loyalties to you. Once you get them to do that." She stood up. "You have them kill off any muthafucka' that you even think is Jamaican. I mean you run through New York with an intense hatred like never before. The more of them you kill off, the weaker his army will become, and soon another head will rise in Jamrock, and King will be old news." She sat back down.

"But, Pops, always told me that the only way a new head can rise is if the old one dies first."

She shrugged her shoulders. "It's either him or you." She gave me a menacing stare. In two days, you will receive a hundred kilos of pure China White from Grenada, then, the next day, you'll get a hundred kilos of pure Peruvian flake, pink fish scale. You must go hard with these shipments, they will come along with artillery, and explosives. It is time that you rise as a king and do away with the old days of being a defenseless pussy under your father." She slapped me hard. "You are a warrior. I raised you. You have more of my blood in you than you do him. Listen to me!" She grabbed me by the throat. "I will kill you if you lose this war to him or any other man. You hear me?"

My nose began to bleed. I sniffed the blood back inside it. "Yes, ma'am." I pulled her to me and held her for ten minutes in silence while she cried on my shoulder.

"No woman should have to choose between her husband and son. Tasia could never love with this form of understanding. We are different. You are different. You two can only love each other once you have been through something and made it. Life for the both of you is about to get really real over the next month or so. Trust me on this."

Chapter 10

It was two o'clock in the morning, when Tasia turned on the lamp beside our bed and sat up with her back against the headboard. "Daddy, are you awake?"

Because of the long discussions me and my mother had together, I chose to lay down this night with two pistols tucked into my holsters and a bulletproof vest across my chest that she'd given me before I left her home.

"Yeah, boo." I rubbed my eyes and sat up next to her. "What it do?"

"Well, I don't wanna make you feel a way or anything, but there's some things on my heart that I need to get off, or I feel like I will never be able to sleep again. Would you mind if I tell you what they are?"

"Sure, baby, what's eating you?" My stomach growled loud as hell, which was odd because we'd just eaten a few hours prior, though not a lot because of the way my mother had treated Tasia which is why my Queen had sent us home with all the leftovers.

"I was thinking about some of the things your mother was saying about how you must not feel a specific way about me. I would be lying if I didn't say that I was hurt real bad. I really like you, and my insecurities within myself is making me feel like I'm not good enough to be with you. Can you kinda tell me what she picked up on that I didn't? I mean do you really care about me?"

I was quiet for a moment. "Damn, baby, you woke me up for this right here? I thought you had something else on your mind." I laughed and squeezed her thick thigh.

She snatched her leg away from me. "I'm serious."

I placed both of my big hands over my face and kept them there for a moment. When I removed them, I was looking at the ceiling with a loss for words. "Check dis' out, baby. I care about you, and there is no reason for you to feel so insecure."

"You can't tell me how to feel, Tyson. I am all screwed up, right now. Your mother knows you way better than I do, and she's basically telling me that I don't have any chance with you long term. Do you have any idea how that made me feel?" Her eyes got watery. She blinked and wiped her face full of tears before I could see them clearly.

I put my arm around her neck. "Tasia, listen."

She pushed my arm away and jumped out of the bed. "No, Tyson, I need to know what you feel about me, right now! Stop saying that you care. Stop beating around the bush and tell me what's good. I am so for real."

I scooted out of the bed and stepped in front of her. "Tasia, it's me and you, boo. Can't you see that I ain't in the streets fuckin' wit' nobody else? If I ain't in the trenches on some hustling shit, then I'm in this mafuckin' house wit' you. That should tell you everything you need to know right there."

She nodded her head. "Yeah, it should, but it don't. I need to hear the words out of your mouth. And why is it so hard for you to love me, anyway, huh? Is it cause I ain't as yellow as, Ashlynn, huh? What, you racist against my complexion or whatever?"

"What?"

"Nigga, you heard me. Why don't you wanna love me? What's the matter with me? Tell me, I'm a big girl, I can take it." She wiped tears off her face.

"Ain't nothin' wrong wit' you. Damn, Ma, yo' lil' ass is perfect. I mean that shit."

She poked me in the chest with her finger. "Nigga, you are a whole ass lie. If I was perfect, you would love me already. But it's all good, though. If you don't love me, then I don't love yo' black ass either. I don't care how fine you are no more either." She turned her back to me and braced herself. Then she grabbed a pillow from the bed and stormed out of the room. "I'm sleeping on the couch. Lying next to you is hurting my heart. I can't handle this rejection."

I sat on the edge of the bed, speechless, and sleepy. I knew the right thing to do was to go in there and chase after her, but instead. I stayed on the edge of the bed for another hour, before I climbed into it, and slowly fell asleep with a heavy heart for her and determined to take over Brooklyn.

***

The next day, I was up at five in the morning, motivated, and ready to get on bidness. Maze pulled up to the house driving a Mazda truck, when I slipped into the passenger's seat of the whip, he yawned and placed his fist over his mouth. Then he looked over at me and shook his head.

"Tyson, what the fuck you got us up this early in the morning for?" He asked, yawning again. This time he didn't cover his mouth.

"Yo', it's time to turn up around this mafucka. I got some major shipments coming through, and before they drop, we need to make sure Red Hook belongs to us. When I say Red Hook, I'm talking from the borough, all the way across the bay to East Orange, word up."

Maze yawned again and sat up. His eyes were bloodshot. "Now this is the shit I'm talking about. You are hollering that cash shit. I'm all ears, when and where we finna' pick up this drop, and how much?"

"Slow ya roll, Dunn, first thing is first. We're about to run through the borough and find out who's with us, and who's acting like they're against us. Any mafucka that's against us, we're applying pressure right away and moving their ass around before the shipment even gets here. You feel what I'm talkin' bout, bruh?"

Maze picked up his Starbucks cup from the console. "You see this?" He raised the cup to his lips. "Nigga, this is me drinking coffee. That means I'm trying to wake up so we can get on the same page." He closed his eyes and sipped on with steam rising around the side of his face.

I nodded. "Let's move then."

***

One by one, we stopped at each building, and went up and down the floors, knocking on specific doors asking the dope boys inside who they were rolling with? We needed to know if they were going to fall in line, and get on our payroll? Or if we were going to have to move them around? If they promised to roll with us, we let them know we were developing payroll and a system for our hustlers. A system that would be implemented real soon.

I promised them that their money count was about to go up and that under us they would be well taken care of, as well as their families. I also let it be known that any opposing would result in death, immediately. That while we were extending them a hand, and a leg up in the game, we weren't going to hesitate to annihilate them at all costs if shit ever looked funny. Maze stood behind me with one of the evilest mugs I had ever seen on his face. Almost everybody knew about his body count, and how he got down in the streets.

They understood that a killa like him standing behind me meant serious business and that they were doing a deal with reapers because, in Brooklyn, birds of a feather flock together. While I wasn't out there or known as being a cold-blooded killer like Maze the people of our borough knew Maze didn't hang with any men that didn't get down like him, or worse than him. So, they figured I was about that death play, just as much as he was.

We went door to door for hours putting the word out of what was to come, and what was to be expected once we got all the way in motion, and door after door we were met with what seemed like sincere compliance. Ever since the Coronavirus pandemic had hit New York, there had been droughts on the dry drugs that usually came through the city. A lot of the Kingpins were holding their product close to their chest. Anybody fortunate enough to have a plug lacing them the way that me and Maze were about to be lacing our workers were in there. They would be given the opportunity to rise above other dope boys that had been in the game longer than them, and when it came to the hustling world, elevation was everything.

We were about ninety-five percent done with the Red Hook Houses when we got over to Verona Street and came upon the 9th Floor. I stepped off the landing first and came into the hallway that was packed with fifteen dudes. All of them had blue bandanas on their faces. They stood so that the entire hallway was blocked. There was one member of the crowd that was more out front than the rest. He was about five-feet-eight inches tall, dark-skinned, and slim with clothes on so tight I wondered how he was able to have the big Mach-90 sticking out of his waistband the way that it was.

Maze went ahead of me. "Yo', I see what this is already. That's BB and his Blue Note crew. Fuck up, niggas? What, we have a problem or sum'?" Maze upped his shirt to show off his two F&N weapons with the extended clips.

We were rolling eight deep, so our young crew of savages came to stand behind Maze. I was already imagining which one of the niggas I was gon' hit first. I had my eyes set on BB, and the two dudes behind him that had shotguns in their hands. I stepped beside Maze but kept my silence. I wasn't the talking type. I let my guns speak for me.

BB stepped forward again. "Say, cuz', I heard y'all was going door to door asking mafuckas if they gon' roll wit' y'all when y'all buss whatever move you're about to. I don't give a fuck about what you dudes finna' do, as long as you leave the Verona buildings to the gang." BB looked back at his crew.

I stepped into his line of vision now. "n'all, Blood, Red Hook is for the taking. We ain't about to do the thing where we are breaking off sections and rendering them to other crews. You niggaz either gon' roll wit' the clan, or we deading shit right here and right now."

All along the hallway, the only sound that was heard was guns cocking. That sound made my heart beat faster. My adrenalin began to flow, I felt giddy.

"What, nigga. First, of all, we don't even know you. Who is this nigga, Maze? Talking like we some hoes or somethin'? You betta tell him about the crew's body of work. Let this nigga know what he getting himself into before we have to knock that head off his shoulders, cuz', straight up." He looked me up and down, then looked over at Maze.

Maze laughed. "Body of work, between twenty of you niggas, you might have ten bodies. That's a bad month for me. Far as my man's go. Yo', I ain't gotta speak. Blood can speak for himself."

"Yeah, well, this is what it is. We been hustling on Verona Street since we were kids. We ain't trying to move North, South, East, or West. We're staying right here, and we ain't running under nobody but ourselves. You niggas can gon' head-on with that dumb shit, and leave Verona off the list of your take over. That's in your best interest. If not, then it looks like we're about to go to war, and you already know my brother, Kano, will come home in six months. You know what he do." BB pulled his nose. "So, what we finna do?"

"Yo', name, BB, right? You run this building and shit?" BB grunted. "Yeah, nigga, what about it?"

"You niggas getting money wit' him?" I asked looking over his shoulder.

He blocked my vision from them. "Don't address my hittas'. Ain't shit moving. Not wit' my buildings, my block, my niggas, Verona period. So, step off. Y'all leave that shit across the busy street. I run this."

I laughed and nodded. "Yeah, my nigga?"

"Yeah, cuz'. This is what it is," BB returned.

"n'all, bitch, dis' is what it is." I pressed the .44 Desert Eagle to his forehead and pulled the trigger. *Boom!*

His brains blew out the back of his head. His dome jerked backward. He dropped his guns, and took two steps forward, before falling to his knees in front of Maze. I didn't look down. I aimed at the first of the two dudes that I had already made my mind up about popping before. I gave them two face shots apiece while they were still looking down at BB in shock. They twisted and fell beside him. The rest of his crew took off running down the hall. Maze and our shooters took off behind bussing their guns back-to-back. I stepped over, BB, and blew two more holes into his face, after rolling him over. I needed for his kill to be heinous. The more gruesome, the louder my name would ring through the borough. It was time for me to emerge as my own king, and blood had to be shed to cement my foundation in Brooklyn.

***

After it was all said and done, I felt we'd made a good lead way. It was one in the morning by the time Maze pulled up in front of my duplex and stopped his truck. We shook up, and I was about to get out when he stopped me. "Say, Dunn, I already know we're about to get this money in a major way. That both me and you are about to go down in the slums as legends. But we're missing one thing, Money."

I frowned at him. "Oh, yeah, B, what's that?" The Mach-11 on my hip was sticking in my waist. It made me feel so uncomfortable.

"A name, son. Yo', we wilding, but a mafucka ain't got a crew's name to stick our work to."

"Yeah, they do, kid. I just ain't put that shit out there yet. But it's already written across my heart." I positioned my fully automatic so that the barrel stopped cutting into me. "In all things you do, you must be a king. We are trapping, we are going to be the kings of that shit. So, we're gonna emerge as the Trap Kings."

Maze repeated the name over and over. He slowly began to nod. "The Trap Kings, I like that, B, word up. Yo', it's official then. We the kings of the trap, son. That's peace." He nodded his head in a what up fashion. "Say, Dunn, I liked that move you pulled on, BB. That was live. I got you forever, my nigga. Word to God." Were his last words before he pulled off and left me standing there ready for a hostile takeover of first Brooklyn, then New York as a whole.

Chapter 11

When the shipment hit, we went into overdrive plugging specific buildings with just the right amount of product. I made sure I put the potent Heroin into the hands of the dope boys that were starving and looking for a way to prove themselves to me by grinding as hard as they could. Before the product was placed into their hands, I befriended their mothers and sisters. I bought outfits for their children, and baby mothers. I walked through their project apartments and put groceries in their places before I laid down the law. Once an understanding was met, I entrusted them with the product that was guaranteed to get all of us rich.

The hustlers I trusted the least were given cell phones, and cheap whips, to drive around with a certain amount of coke at a time making drop-offs to customers who called the Trap Kings and paid using a cash app. I didn't allow no money to touch these young dudes' hands. I made sure I stayed on top of each buy and sell, and at the end of every week, I had the treasurer of our crew pay the runners a weekly salary of thirty-five hundred, which was more than any other dope boy was getting for doing something so minimal all-around New York.

Maze played the role of enforcer. He went behind me and made sure everything was running smooth. Whenever things seemed out of sorts on the dope boys' ends he checked that shit it. He handed out severe beatings and took lives, all in the name of business and dominance. He made sure that before each punishment, he allowed the person to know that I have given him the go-ahead to handle his business. Then he would screw them over in a fashion that quickly made it all over the borough.

Within two months, our operations were up and running strong. I was able to maintain control with an iron fist. The money began to come so fast that I became shell shocked. I had never seen so much money in all my life. It was easy to get overwhelmed because even though the cash was coming like crazy, my staff was over a thousand people that I needed to pay, and kept fed, as well as myself, and Maze. Even though I was good with numbers, I needed help, and that's where Tasia stepped in and got shit right in order. She seemed to be a whiz with the numbers.

She found a system that worked for both of us, and she was even able to tell me where it looked like something funny was taking place in different locations, and at different times. Because of her, I was able to monitor, and stay on top of things more easily.

***

In the fourth month, things sped up dramatically. Brooklyn started to look brand new with members of my crew that were once forced to drive around the city in old cars, with bad paint jobs, and busted interiors, they were now rolling newly released foreign whips fresh off the showroom floor. The rims were the biggest and shiniest. The interiors were plush, and the music banged the loudest. When my young hustlers stepped out of their cars and trucks, their necks were flooded in jewelry, along with their wrists, and ear lobes. Their jeans were fitted tight, but the bulges of cash were easily made out to the eye. They carried themselves with a certain swag. A swagger that said they had come from nothing, and now they were getting stupid cash.

Maze was more laid back. He'd come from the field of being an extreme jack boy, and he was exactly that at heart. He kept it simple. He rocked all-black hoodies with Gucci jeans, and a pair of Jordan's almost every day. His cars were clean but regular. They didn't have any rims on them, and his sound system could only be heard once you got inside of his whip. He had his style, and even with large sums of cash, he was sticking to it.

Me, I wasn't trying to hear none of that. I copped me a newly released, black on black Ferrari truck with the all-burgundy leather interior, and had that bitch banging so loud that I wore earplugs when I drove it. My rims were thirty-two inches of solid gold, and I wore so much jewelry that I felt weighed down half the time. Everything was designer. The leather seats of my Ferrari were even styled by Chanel. I had five whips, and all those bitches were fly.

***

When I came into the house, in the second week of the fifth month of our hustling season Tasia was sitting on the couch with a bottle of Ace of Spade in her hand, and four duffle bags filled with cash sitting on the table in front of her. She saw me and held up the bottle.

"Don't get on my nerves, Tyson. I ain't got around to counting this yet. I just put five of these same-sized bags in the safe, and just when I thought I was about to get some sleep, Maze brought me these. Don't you think we got enough money, yet?"

I took off my Roberto Cavalli leather jacket and dropped it on the couch beside her. I leaned down to give her a kiss, and all four platinum iced chains hit her in the forehead before my lips could even touch her. I held them out of the way. The light in the room reflected off the diamond rings on my fingers. "Yo', you telling me that as my Queen, you feel like we got enough money already? Say word?" I kissed her soft lips. Damn, they were juicy.

She kissed me and leaned back. "I don't know, Daddy. We getting bags like these every day. Damn, are you leaving money for anybody else in New York? I ain't saying that to be cute, I'm really asking you this as a serious question?" I laughed. "n'all, fuck them, B. It's all about this king of the trap shit." I picked up my coat and pulled out a box from Harry Winston. I kneeled. "Speaking of which, I picked this lil' number up for you today. I saw Beyonce rocking something like this at the Grammys, and I wanted to make sure that you was killing her shit."

Tasia took the box and opened it to reveal an iced, yellow lemonade female Patek watch. There were so many diamonds on it, and all over it that it looked like a bunch of glitter. Her eyes lit up. "Oh, my God, it's so pretty." She smiled brightly and looked over at me. "Thank you, Tyson. Daddy, you're always spoiling me." She hugged my neck.

I hugged her for a second and made her stand up. "Yo', Tasia, I just gotta say I appreciate you, Boo. Do you hear me?"

She looked into my eyes. "Yes, Daddy, but why are you saying this?"

"Because, Boo, it's plenty niggas that's out here getting money, that's using their jewels to master this game, but they ain't giving her no just do. That shit ain't finna be me. I already know I couldn't do none of this without you. I got that hustle shit down pact, but you're the brains, Boo. That's why I gotta give you your props and appreciation." I kissed her forehead.

She stomped her right foot. "Aw, Daddy, you're about to make me emotional. You already know you be having a hard time when I get like that."

I shook my head. "n'all, cutie, it's good. I know you're a female and all that. If you wanna express ya self through emotions, word to Jehovah, yo', I'm here wit' you." I kissed her soft lips and gripped that ass. She was wearing a pair of tight Fendi stretch pants and the material made it feel as if I was already touching her regular, warm skin. It felt good.

"Daddy, when are you planning on stopping, though? Like, do you have a certain number in your head?" She looked into my eyes.

"n'all, I don't, I don't think most hustlers do. I think I wanna ball for as long as time allows me to. What's wrong with that?" I went in for a kiss.

She pulled her head back and stepped away from me. She hugged her body. "You know what, I wasn't going to say anything, but I just gotta be honest with you. The way you've been carrying on, and makes me feel like you really don't know what you're doing past a hustling or getting money standpoint."

I frowned. "What are you talking about now?" How the fuck had I just given her an iced Patek, and she was coming at me with this dumb shit?

"What you don't understand it seems is that all of what you're doing has already been done before. And nine times out of ten, the outcome is always the same. Either, the hustler winds up in prison for a long time. Or they wind up dead. Either way, the system will allow you to ball for a second, before it crushes you like the worthless *nigger* it sees you as. The only reason you are able to do what you are doing is so that you can trick and misguide as many of our young brothers and sisters as you can. Once they become brainwashed into thinking that this way is the only way to make it out of Brooklyn, then your job for those powers that be up top is over and they are coming for you."

Now she had me lost. "Who? What the fuck are you talking about?"

"The feds, Uncle Sam, America, whatever. What you need to do is develop a plan so that this part of your life is short but beneficial for the long term. You gotta be different, and you have to be smarter. *We* have to be smarter. The money is coming in by the truckload. Let's use it wisely and get out of the game. Please, because I love you, and I'm pregnant." She came over and kissed me on the cheek. "Now take a seat and think about that." She walked out of the room without glancing back at me.

I sat on the couch and dropped my head. The things that she said began to run rampant through my mind. Pregnant? How far along, and when did this happen. Also, was I being stupid in the game? Was the feds coming for me already? I thought hustlers got at least a five-year run. Maybe she was overreacting. I needed clarity. I got up and headed behind her.

"Tasia, bring yo' ass here. You think you gon' just say that shit, and don't have to explain yourself?" I walked into the living room, spotted her and my heart damned near leaped out of my chest. "What the fuck?!"

Chapter 12

Kammron held Tasia against the wall with a shotgun to her cheek. He pumped it and smiled at me. "What it do, kid? I heard about how you balling and all of that shit now. That's what's up? Seems like you snatching up everythang that you ever wanted, including some shit that don't even belong to you. Like this bitch, right here." He gripped her ass. "Fuck you got to say 'bout dis'?"

There were four men with him. They wore black ski masks. Their eyes were red and appeared menacing.

I held my ground. "Kammron, dis' what it is, huh? After a nigga gunned yo' ass down. You come back at me over a bitch. Say word, Boss, I thought yo' legend was bigger than that." I laughed him off.

He lowered his eyes at me. "What, you mean to tell me you been fuckin' this bitch for damn near a year now, and you don't give a fuck about her. Wow, Tasia, and I bet you been calling him Daddy and all that shit." He laughed and flung her to the ground. He placed the barrel against her cheek. "Kid, on Harlem, I'll splash this bitch with no regard. You betta act like you give a fuck, or on my borough this bitch is dead." He held the gun with two hands and bit into his bottom lip.

"Fuck you, nigga. Do what you gotta do. This shit is part of the game." I made sure that I leaned on my panic button that was right next to the light switch in the living room. I felt my elbow press it inward.

"Please don't kill me, Kammron. I'm sorry, I don't know what I did to you, but I'm sorry. Please don't take my life, I'm pregnant," Tasia cried.

"What, by dis' nigga? Really? Aw hell n'all." He leaned down and squeezed her cheeks together before he eased the barrel into her mouth. "Bitch you played me. I don't know what the fuck you thought this was, but you got a nigga? Where the fuck is your mother? You betta have the right answer." He eased the barrel out of her mouth again.

"I don't know. I swear to God, I don't," Tasia swore. Tears ran down her cheeks.

Now I was feeling some type of way. "Yo', she don't go nowhere, Blood. Fuck you jaded wit' her for? Ain't you done enough?"

"n'all, nigga, you ain't even seen the half of what I can do. This bitch mama hit me for three million last night and disappeared. I wanna know where she is, and where is my money. Not only am I about to strip yo' punk ass of everything you got, but I'm gon' knock this lil' bitch's brains out of her head if she don't tell me what I wanna know. Where the fuck is, Jazzy?"

"I don't know, I swear!" Tasia screamed.

"Yeah, bitch, well I bet you gon' tell me if I do this." He aimed his shotgun at me and smiled.

Just then two red beams appeared on his forehead. I smiled. Maze came from the back of the house with two .45s. "Bitch, didn't she just say that she didn't know, huh? Rapist ass nigga. Back the fuck up before I smoke you, word to Brooklyn. The borough will have a celebration like we just won the NBA championship."

Kammron backed up and placed his hands at shoulder length. "Nigga, you whack me, and I whack his punk ass sister, and your daughter, Lexi. Yeah, bitch nigga, that's right I got both of those hoes." He smirked.

"Lexi? How the fuck you get my baby girl? Nigga, you bluffing," Maze dared him. "You ain't that stupid.

"Big bad, Maze, having all this new money. You got safe houses all over Brooklyn. Your name ringing bells all the way to Harlem. Yet, you can't afford decent security for your daughter, and you got her moms' living in the Harlem River Houses. Bum ass nigga, when your chips get right the first people you move out are supposed to be the women, goofy. Pull that trigger and my niggas fuck the shit out of her for three days straight, before they torture and kill her. We don't give a fuck that she only eight. Word up. Dis is Harlem, right here."

Maze swallowed. "Yo', fuck you want wit' my baby, kid? She's just a child."

"Aw, so now you're getting choked up. I see this is gon' be fun. I can't believe I choked up a killa!" He mugged me. "Bitch, yo' sister on her last legs. I want my three million from Jazzy and I want three million from the so-called Kings of the Trap." He laughed at the top of his lungs. "That shit still tickles me. Make it happen. Y'all got two weeks." He eased backward.

Maze kept the beams on him. "Fuck is Lexi man? Where is my baby?" He bit into his bottom lip.

Kammron stopped and trailed his eyes up the beams that were on him. He mugged Maze with serious hatred and irritation. "Yo', you think this shit a game or somethin', my nigga? I done already told you what it is wit' ya Lexi, and ya still gon' keep ya joints aimed at me like it's sweet?" He stepped up closer to him and looked from one gun unto the next. "Nigga, put them hammers down before I drop that lil' bitch."

Instead of putting them down, Maze raised them and bit into his lower lip. I could tell he wanted to waste Kammron all over my living room floor. "Yo, you finna' have to show me proof that you got my baby, nigga. Ain't no hoes over here. Show me proof or yo' niggas finna' pick you up off the floor. Word up."

Kammron snickered. He nodded at one of his hittas. They stepped over to Maze and showed him a cellphone. Maze lowered his guns, and his face began to look as if he was about to throw up. He backed beside me.

Kammron smiled. "That's the reaction I was looking for. This six-million dollars total. You can cut the payment in half if you find Jazzy and have her drop my cheese. If you don't, both of you niggas gon' find these bitches piece by piece. You mafuckas wanna be in the trenches, well, I'm finna' show y'all that ain't no crew more heavily in the trenches than the Coke Kings. We run New York. He dropped a cellphone on the couch. Answer this bitch when I call it. And no funny bidness." He backed out of the house and disappeared.

As soon as he did, Maze dropped to his knees. "Fuck man, my baby girl. I don't give a fuck about nothing else in this world other than Lexi man. That's my heart." He lowered his head to his chest.

I helped Tasia come to her feet. She slapped my hands away. "What the fuck is wrong with you, Tyson?" She hollered.

I was stuck. "What are you talking about? I'm just trying to help yo' ass up."

"You could've gotten me, and this baby killed. Don't you know that Kammron hates my fuckin' guts? And you're gonna go and play with him? You damned near dared him to pull the trigger and take me out? So, yeah, what the fuck is wrong with you?"

I waved her off. "Man, that nigga wasn't gon' blow you. He knew that if he smoked you, I was going to smoke him. I put that heat to his ass already. He ain't trying to feel those shots again. Trust me on that. That nigga was bluffing. Calm yo' lil' ass down."

"Calm down? Really? You're telling me to calm down?" She laughed as if she was hurt. Then she walked up to me and pushed me with two hands. "He just had a fuckin' shotgun down my throat, and you're gonna tell me to calm down. n'all, Tyson, you need to get a grip. This shit is serious."

Maze stood up and looked as if he were drained. "Yo', I don't know what I'm finna do, but I can't see myself paying this nigga no three million. At the same time, I can't lose my daughter either. I'm fucked up, right now." He lowered his head and picked up the cellphone. "What are you going to do about, Hermes?"

I came over and sat across from him. "I don't know. I guess the first thing we should try and do is locate Jazzy. If she got three million of that nigga's money that'll cut our burden in half. If we don't, that six about to be major. I don't even think we got six stacked just yet."

"I know we don't, and even if we did, that shit ain't about to go to the Coke Kings. Fuck Harlem. This is Brooklyn, nigga. Red Hook, Brooklyn at that. There has to be a way to get our people back, and not give that fool one penny. I can't even think, right now, but I'm sure it's gon' come to me. We got a few days to get shit right." His eyes became watery. "She just eight-man, damn that bitch ass nigga." He hid his face with his hand and walked out of the front door. "I'll be in touch, Tyson. I gotta go get my ducks in a row and find out how this nigga managed to get my Princess." He slammed the door.

Tasia came into the living room. "Tyson, your mother is on the phone. She says that it is an emergency."

T.J. Edwards

Chapter 13

My mother paced back and forth with her fists balled up. She stopped in front of me as I sat on her living room sofa. She looked down and into my eyes. "Your sister may be dead already, Tyson. The last time that I saw her, she looked so bad I couldn't stand to stare at her. She is fading away, and I didn't know what to do before Kammron and the Coke Kings took her away."

"So, what are you saying, mama? You're still not telling me what I should do."

She shrugged her shoulders. "Kammron is asking for six million dollars, right?"

"Yeah, that's what he said. But he said that the money can be cut in half if we can find Ms. Jazzy."

She sat next to me on the sofa. "As a mother, I have never felt sicker or more afraid, than when I witnessed the state of Hermes. I never thought either of my children would have ever succumbed to the grips of Heroin or any hard drug. She is my baby, and while I know that she has been through a lot, I can't help but feel as if she is weak for falling into the abyss. The last time that I saw her she was less than a hundred pounds. Her face was sunken in. She was on her way out." She stood up. "So, no, you're going to keep doing what you do, and we aren't giving Kammron a dime. Instead, we are going to apply pressure to the Coke Kings in a way that they have never seen before. I have already arranged for some of my island men to come to New York and back you. I will brief them on the situation. After that, they will be solely under your command until we crush Kammron and his Harlem idiots. We have to make this fast because I am told the war between your father and Garvey is coming to a close. King seems to be winning, and he has already said that once it is over, he is coming for his son that turned his back on him. That's you. You must be ready to stand guard against him, and handle your business as a man. I have the utmost faith in you, son."

I nodded my head. "But, Ma, I can't just let this Kammron nigga take Hermes out the game. That's my sister? I love her. How can you let go so easily?"

"But I'm not, Hermes is among the walking dead, son. I would rather her go without me having to see her dwindle away than to watch it take place day by day right before my eyes. I am strong, but that would shatter me. Besides, six million dollars going into the bank account of a rival enemy is foolish. Sometimes when it comes to war, we just lose a few to come out victorious. This is one of those times. Proceed with the mission to lockdown Red Hook. I will do my part. I love you, son." She kissed my cheek and walked out of the huge media room of the mansion.

I was lost, and I felt like for the first time in my life my mother was telling me the wrong thing to do. How could a mother give up on her own child? How could a mother say that a bill is too high to pay for her baby? Or how could a mother say she'd rather watch her child die from afar, rather than right in her arms?

I was lost and broken, and one thing was for sure, there was no way I could accept her advice and give up on Hermes. I didn't care if she was a hundred and fifty pounds or five pounds. I was coming for my sister. There was no way I was about to allow Kammron to kill her because I was found to be inadequate. n'all, I owed, Hermes, more than that.

***

"Yo', check this shit out, B. That's six million dollars right there," Maze said, dropping the fourth duffel bag by my foot as we stood on the rooftop of one of the buildings right along Coffey Street. He had on all-black with his hoodie pulled over his head. He smoked on a Newport back-to-back as if he was nervous and afraid.

"How the fuck you come up with six million dollars in a week, nigga? What, you been pulling kick doors or some shit?" I asked kneeling down and unzipping one of the bags? I held up a stack of money and looked it over closely.

"n'all, B, I had to holler at a few of my Asian homies to make it do what it do." Maze flicked the cigarette over the edge of the building.

I took a marker and trailed it down the face of the hundred-dollar bill. It bled and turned gray. I mugged him. "Nigga, this ain't that. This shit is fake." I stood up, holding the money in my hand. I did the same thing to another bill. This time it took longer to turn, but it did eventually. "Yo', you know this shit ain't real, kid?"

Maze snatched the money out of my hand. "Yeah, fool, I know dat'. But Kammron ain't gon' get a chance to do all of that. As soon as I see Lexi, word to Jehovah, man. I'm smoking that nigga, B. Kid gon' play wit' my seed? n'all, fuck that! I gotta have the breath coming out of his lungs."

I stepped back and shook my head. "So, how you wanna go about this shit? Nine times out of ten he gon' want the money before he releases our people. If that's the case, we run the risk of him looking the cash over and finding out that it's fake. Once he does that, he can smoke both of them, and we won't be able to do shit. Do you think it'll be smarter if we use at least a million of real cash, and the rest can be fake?"

Maze eyes lit up. "Damn, nigga, I didn't even think of that. That way he could go over the first bag and see that everything is on the up and up. He'd release my daughter, and that's when we'd knock that nigga's head off."

"Yeah, Blood, in that order. But I was thinking that we fill all the bags with the top layer of real money, and the bottom could be that fake shit. That way if he decides to pick random bags it won't bite us in the ass."

Maze rubbed his temples in a circular motion with his eyes closed. "Yo, Dunn, I ain't slept since my kid got napped. Word up. You seem to be firing on all cylinders. So, I'ma let you run the show. All I ask is that you let me know what exactly it is that we are doing step by step that way I can be in tune with you. All I want is my little girl back? And to personally torture and murder that bitch ass nigga. I ain't asking for much." He stood in my face.

"Yo', I ain't a weak nigga. There is very few things that can bring me to my knees. But, Lexi is my baby. She is the love of my life. I can't let nothin' happen to her. I don't even wanna think about that nigga having his nasty ass hands all over my seed, B. Damn, this shit fucking me up," his voice started to crack. He slumped his head, and when he looked back up at me tears were running down his cheeks.

"Bruh, I need you to think for me right now because I can't do it. I need you to finesse this situation so that I get my baby back. I can't focus on shit else but that, right now. You see these bags under my eyes and shit. Kid, I'm lost." He held my shoulders and cried right there in front of me.

I couldn't do anything but swallow the lump in my throat. I had never seen a grown man cry before, especially not a cold-blooded killer. For as long as I had known Maze he had always been so tough. So rough, and rugged. The fact that he stood there on the verge of a nervous breakdown told me he was falling apart over Lexi. I knew I had to be the brains of the operation, and I would.

"Say, B, I got you. We got this. I'ma make sure we bring ya jewel home. So, hold ya' head." I pulled him to me, and we hugged while our troops stood behind us on security.

From the vantage point on the roof, we could see all Red Hook all the way to the bay and across to East Orange, New Jersey. The world, our world, was cold and attacking at every moment. Only true kings could ever crush and conquer it, and if we were to do both it started with me.

"Yo', I know you got me, Dunn. I know you ain't gon' let my baby fall by the wayside. I appreciate you. I'll lie, steal and kill for you, too. For the rest of my life, Tyson. That's my word." He hugged me tight and dropped to one knee. "Fuck!" Just the sight of seeing this gave me the motivation to go into overdrive for my homey, and for both Hermes and Lexi.

***

That night when I got home Tasia was stuffing two suitcases with her clothes. When she saw me come into the room, she ignored me and kept on going from the closet to the suitcases that were on top of the bed, stuffing them with her things. There was already one suitcase in the living room.

"What are you doing, Shorty?" I asked, standing at the doorway of the bedroom.

"I'm packing my things, so I can leave. I can't do this anymore." She opened the dresser drawers and proceeded to take the things out of them, loading them into the open suitcases.

I stood there for a moment before I walked further into the room. "You can't do what anymore?"

"This, Tyson. Us. You and me. I can't do it anymore. It's fuckin' me up, mentally, and physically," she said without even looking at me.

"So, you just finna' give up, and throw in the towel on us? Really?"

"To be honest with you, Tyson, I don't even think there has ever been an us. I can't get it out of my mind what you did last week. Kammron coulda taken my life, and that would have been that. You didn't even try to save me, and every woman loves to know that she has a savior. She might not depend on him, or go to him to be saved, but she likes to know that if ever she needed to be saved, he got her." She jumped on to the bed and sat on a suitcase before zipping it up. Then she jumped off and got to going back and forth again.

"Yo', you talking 'bout saving? I'm the nigga that saved ya' ass the first time when he tried that dumb shit wit' you. I'm the one that popped him up and left his ass twisted on the pavement. That was me, and I did that shit for you."

"Yeah, you did that. And I appreciated that then, and I appreciate it now. But he could have still killed me only a week ago. Where would that have left us?" She rubbed her stomach.

My eyes trailed down to her hand. "Yo', you ain't about to go no muthafuckin' where. You belong to me, and I ain't going. We are about to figure this shit out. Stop all this extra shit and put those clothes back in the closet. Come on, hurry up." I snapped my fingers at her.

She stood in place and pinned her gaze on the floor. "Tyson, I am ready to leave. I need some space, and I need to create some distance from this whole thing for myself, and for this baby, I am carrying. I need you to allow me to do that."

"Shorty, you ain't going no muthafuckin' where without me. Matter of fact, you ain't leaving this house." I grabbed the suitcases, threw them all back into the closet, and closed the door loudly.

Tasia stood with her arms at her sides and her eyes closed. "What are you doing? You can't do this."

"I can, and I am, Tasia, damn. Why the fuck you always gotta make a nigga go to the extreme and shit. Why can't I just love you, and have my woman? You're all I got, right now and I ain't about to allow you to take yourself away from me because I need you, Boo. Damn, I need yo' ass, and I love you. I love you with all my mafuckin' heart." I started to shake because I felt so weak, angry, and vulnerable. I had never felt all these emotions at one time.

Tasia had her mouth covered with a smile on her pretty face. She removed her hand briefly. "What did you just say, Daddy?"

"That I love you and I need you. That you are my heart." I took a deep breath and blew it out.

"Do you mean that?"

"Hell yeah, I do. I can't be without you, Boo. I don't know what the fuck I'm about to step into, all I know is that I ain't trying to step into it without you by my side. I'm sorry about last week. You already know I'd kill that nigga over you in a heartbeat. I'm just sorry, baby." My eyes teared up, and I felt weak as a bitch. I tried to turn my back on her.

She stopped me and stepped in front of me. She held my face in her hands. "It's okay, baby. I love you, too, and whatever you are about to step into, I will be right here holding you down. You are my king. I love you with all my heart and all I've ever wanted was to hear you say those three words. That meant everything to me." She wrapped her arms around my neck and kissed my lips. "I'd die for you, Tyson. I'd die for you with no hesitation."

We continued to kiss. I held her small waist and looked into her eyes. "I'm sorry, boo, from here on out I'ma appreciate you more. Don't be trying to leave me and shit. I need you. You are the purest form of love outside of my mother that I have ever known, and I am thankful for you. I mean that."

Tasia stomped both of her feet and shook her head. "Fuck this. I want some of my daddy, right now. You got my girl parts leaking." She hopped on me and wrapped her thighs around my waist.

I laughed and caught her. "Yo', I'm finna' wear this ass out."

Chapter 14

Tasia pushed me back on the bed and straddled my body. She'd already pulled off my shirt and slipped my pants off. Her hands roamed all over me. She bit into my neck and sucked on it. "I love you so much, Daddy. I swear to God I do. You are my heart and my soul." She bit all over me before she sucked ever so lovely.

"I love you, too, Boo. Damn, I love my thick ass baby." I grabbed her ass and squeezed that mafucka. There was a thin strip of cloth that separated her backside. Her flesh was nice and warm. I could feel her pussy moving up and down my stomach, and it made me shiver. Looking into her eyes was like I was seeing her for the first time. I was crazy about this woman, and even though we were young, I couldn't see myself being without her. I felt like I needed her. Imagining her leaving me was enough to drive me absolutely crazy. I rolled her over so that she was on her back. Once there, I pulled her tank top over her head and exposed her perfect titties.

I took the beauties in my hand and massaged them. "You're so perfect, baby. Damn, yo' lil' ass is so perfect. I'd kill a nigga over you with no thought to it. You belong to me. Do you understand that?"

"Yes, Daddy." She opened her thighs wider.

I wrapped my right hand around her throat and applied just a bit of pressure. "You ever try to leave me, Tasia, I'ma kill yo ass. You are my baby. We in this it together. Me and you, boo. Us? Don't fuckin' play wit' me." I squeezed harder.

She arched her back and gagged. I released it a bit. "You belong to me too then. You ain't finna say I belong to you, and

I ain't got no stake in you." She smacked my hand away. "'Sides that, you don't own me."

"Oh, yeah?"

"Yeah." She tried to get up. I started shaking. I imagined her leaving me, and I grew angry and jealous. Tasia had my head gone and I didn't even understand how. All I knew was that I needed her and imagining losing her was enough to drive me insane." I pushed her back on the bed and grabbed her neck again.

"So, you gon' play wit' me, huh? You gon' try and take my baby away from me?" I squeezed her neck hard and rubbed my other hand in between her thighs. Her panty front was packed with pussy and appeared damp. I rubbed up and down it, and in between the lips while she struggled to get up.

"You don't love me, Tyson. You don't and you don't own me." She was barely able to get the words out before I tightened my grip. She started to fight me.

I held her down. "I'll die without you, Tasia. You think you're the only one that's crazy, huh? You don't think I'm nuts about yo' ass?" I got into position between her legs and lined myself up. It took me a second, but after some side-to-side action, I slipped into her pussy and dove inch after inch until I was balls deep in what I now considered my box. I cocked back and started fucking her harder than I ever had before. That cat was juicy and wet.

She opened her thighs as wide as she could it seemed. Her back arched. Her nails dug into the sheets on the side of us. She pulled them. "Uh! Uh! Uh! Uh! Daddy! Shit, I love you! Uhhh shit, I love my Daddy!"

I leaned down and choked her with two hands while I pounded into her deeper and deeper. "I'll kill you if you ever leave me. Never baby! This is us!" I hollered and tightened my grip.

Tasia rose her hips up to meet mine. She locked her ankles around my waist and struggled to breathe. Her nails dug into my back and drug down it. Tears welled up in her eyes before they spilled down her cheeks.

I released my hold, and she took in a gasp of air. I kissed and sucked all over her lips. Licking them and running my cheek across them. "This my pussy. This mine. Look at my baby." I looked down and watched my dick go in and out of her at full speed.

She sat up and bit into my shoulder. "Daddy! Daddy! Aww shit, you beating this pussy! You killing yo' lil' mama! Fuccckkk!" She screamed and came all over me.

She fell back and started shaking. Her small hands pushed at my chest.

I grabbed her neck again and started pounding her out with long strokes. "You belong to me, Tasia! Me! I ain't gon' play about you. I ain't gon' ever play about you. I love yo' ass, and I need you for myself. This is us! You hear me?" I released her neck and curled my back again, fucking her harder.

Once again, she took in a deep breath and released it. "Awww fuck, why you doing me like this?! I'm cumming again! I'm cumming! Choke me, Daddy, I need you!"

I grabbed her with two hands around the neck and fucked her up the bed digging and stroking. She wound up pinned against the headboard with me piping her down. I felt her dig her nails into my lower back. I couldn't help cumming deep inside her, jerking like crazy. I pulled my piece out after a while and released the rest all over her pretty stomach and titties, before falling to my side and tonguing her fine ass down. I had become crazy about my woman, and I was ready to kill something over her just to prove myself.

***

After our shower, we laid in bed with her on top of me. Her face was in the crux of my neck, and she kept on lightly humping into me. We were naked and I'd be lying if I said it didn't feel good as heaven. She ran her finger along my lips.

"Tyson, do you really love me as much as you were saying you did before and during our lovemaking session?"

I rubbed her big booty as usual. When a female was as strapped back there as Tasia was, you had to keep yo' hands all over it. "Yeah, boo, I do."

"But what made you suddenly come to that conclusion? What did I do?"

"I don't know." I squeezed her booty. "I guess seeing you ready to walk out of my life like you were going to did something to me. I don't wanna lose you. I don't want you thinking that you don't mean nothin' to me. I would never let that nigga, Kammron hurt you if I could prevent it. I ain't never trying to make you feel like I wouldn't go above and beyond for you because I would."

"n'all, I can't lie. I never thought that you wouldn't, but you know how things go. A girl just wants to feel special, that's all. I didn't like how that whole scene with him played out this time. But I already know that things will be different moving forward." She was quiet for a moment. "Daddy, do you ever think you're going to replace me?"

"Replace you how, what are you talking about?"

"I don't know. You got all this money and all those cars and jewelry. Females gotta be on your heels on a daily basis. I guess I was just wondering if one of them will ever make you throw in the towel with me."

"N'all boo, you and I are forever."

"You promise?"

I nodded. "I promise. I ain't about to let nobody take me away from you. That's why I gotta crush Kammron. Long as that nigga is in the picture, we're going to be worried about being separated." I rubbed her back, then I was right back to gripping that ass again. "Yo', do you really know where your mother is?"

She sat up and brought her knees to her chest. Her pussy popped out from in between them, and as a man, I couldn't help but notice. She began to bite her bottom lip. "Daddy, what if I told you I knew where she was, right now? Would you be mad at me?"

I got up from the bed and looked down at her. "Yo', don't play wit' me, Tasia. Do you really know where yo' moms is?"

She held her silence and bit on the nail of her forefinger. "I might, but I don't wanna say nothing even if I did. All Maze wanna do is kill her. I'm not trying to have nobody hurting my mother, Tyson. Yeah, she hit Kammron's punk ass, but he deserved it. I know what he's going to do once he gets his hands on her, both she and I are terrified. That's why I'm telling you. She told me to tell you what was good because she trusts you. She says that the two of you have a special bond. Whatever that means." She rolled her eyes.

"So, then you do know where she is? And you wanna tell me but you don't want Maze to know that I know where she is? Is that it?"

She climbed out of the bed. "Kammron's so stupid, he thinks she only hit him for three million when she's been tearing him off for a long time. Mama got about seven million in cash from him. She says that she'll be willing to pay you if you can help her get out of Harlem and to Chicago where her family is. She didn't say a number but I'm pretty sure it will be quite a handsome figure. What do you say, Tyson?"

I had never betrayed Maze once since he and I had been jamming. That was my nigga and I didn't give a fuck how much money Ms. Jazzy was trying to hit me wit'. No amount would cause me to turn my back on my homey or keep something like this from him. But I also loved and respected Tasia. Fuck, I was in a catch twenty-two.

"Say, Boo, I'ma help ya' moms off the strength of you. I mean I'ma hit them pockets, too, but just know that me preserving her life, and helping her get out of Harlem is because of you. Where is she?"

Tasia jumped up and down in happiness. "Oh, Daddy, I knew you would come through, I just knew it." She ran to me and hugged my neck tightly. "Okay, so listen to me carefully, because this is the only way we can get her out of her hideout without us being recognized," She began filling me in on everything I needed to know about rescuing, Ms. Jazzy.

Chapter 15

"Kid, I'm praying this nigga ain't got as much common sense as a mafucka give him credit for, B, word up. Son has been a thorn in my side for weeks now. This shit driving me crazy." Maze took a sip from his bottled water. "I saw his moms, Fredricka at Walmart the other day, and every part of me wanted to snatch her ass up to even the score. I figured that would make Kammron turn over our people and all of that, but then I remembered the streets talking saying that he didn't give a fuck about his moms because she smoked that Meth shit now. That would have been an ill-advised move." Maze switched lanes in the Jeep Grand Cherokee we were rolling.

I felt my chest and rubbed my hand over the vest there. "I'm glad you didn't, son. That would have blown our move to the ceiling. Word up, I think we just need to stick to the game plan. Kammron ain't as smart as we give him credit for. At least I can't see it. Plus, Blood, super cocky. He thinks he got the whole world figured out." I smacked a loaded clip into my .45 and cocked it before putting it in the holster under my right arm. I took the other one and did the same thing.

"That's how fuck niggas get their brains knocked out of their heads, too. I'm talking all over the pavement." Maze sat up in his seat. "Yo', on my moms, that nigga ain't never dealt with the kind of animal that I am. He ain't never seen a beast like me before." He looked over at me and shook his head.

"Yeah, I can see that. And only time will tell who's going to be the one to emerge as the king of New York. Once we slay his punk ass, I say we start looking over to Harlem as a new place to open up shop. I hear that nigga making every bit of a million a day just in the Harlem River Houses alone. When it comes to Frederick Douglass Boulevard, kid's doubling his scratch in hours. Harlem seems like it's sweet and those niggas out there ain't as rough as they used to be. The Feds been eating they ass alive."

"Brooklyn run New York, Tyson, word up. We got the hardest niggas, and the baddest hoes. We get the most money. And niggas just ain't seeing the gods, right now. We gotta plow this nigga and reap a harvest. I'm definitely with taking over Harlem. Straight the fuck up." He grabbed a blunt from the ashtray and sparked it. "Now if we could locate that Jazzy bitch, we would really be on to something. Blood says she hit his ass for three million. Nigga for three million I'd run through the white house and take my chances." He laughed and grew serious right away.

I looked out of the window as we drove over the George Washington bridge. "Yeah, three million is a nice chunk of change. But we're in the trenches nigga we'll have that shit in no time. It ain't somethin' we gotta force. We already got a stranglehold on Red Hook."

"That we do." Maze smiled proudly at that. "Dawg, I miss Lexi so much. Last time I saw my baby I'd just taken her shopping and blew a bag on her. I think I mighta dropped every bit of twenty gees and gave her a stack for herself. To us, a gee ain't no money, but when you're eight, that's cream, B. Yo', her eyes lit up like Christmas trees." He shook his head again. "If that rapist ass nigga touched my baby. Fuck!" He slammed his hands on the steering wheel.

"Don't even speak that shit into existence, kid, word up. The power of the tongue is mad crazy. You would be surprised how much shit that wasn't coming your way, suddenly began to come all because you spoke it into existence. So, I don't even think so negative anymore."

"Yeah, well, I can't help it. Blood got a reputation for slaying lil' girls. I know my shorty only eight, but who knows, to that nigga, she might be twenty in his eyes. I swear, God, need to rid the world of niggas like dude. Lil' girls ain't safe no more. Fuck, this some bull shit." He pulled off on the ramp that led us into the heart of Harlem.

I was silent and didn't speak another word. I was lost in deep thought. I took a deep breath as we crossed St. Nicholas and headed over to Lennox. I had never liked, nor fucked with Harlem. From my understanding, the dudes in Harlem were the grimiest. They would sell you something with one hand and dig in your pockets while you were paying for it with their other hand.

In Harlem niggas dated their own aunts and sold dope to their own uncles. They pimped their sisters and popped up their own brothers. Everything in this borough was about making money and annihilating everybody, even your own kin. Harlem was known for no loyalty and blindsided kills. I stayed my distance, and only passed through the borough, I never stopped.

***

Ten minutes later, Kammron was standing at the entranceway to the huge, run down, glass factory. He directed us to drive inside and we did. I saw that he was real deep, with at least ten members of his Coke King Homeys. They stood behind him with jewelry around their necks, and black ski masks on their faces. Kammron was dressed in black and gray fatigues, with black boots laced up. As comical as it seemed, he had four platinum chains around his neck and a gold Glock .40 in his right hand.

Maze pulled into the factory and parked the truck so that our front was facing the entrance way that we came in. He kept the truck running and looked over at me. "Yo', no matter what goes down here, B, I love you, and you, my nigga. Blood in, and Blood out, Dunn. Word to Jehovah man, we brothers." He extended his hand.

I grabbed it and gave him a half hug. "The love is mutual, Dunn, word to the heavens. I'd lose blood for you any day. Blood in, and Blood out." We hugged again, then a serious mug came across my face. I opened the door and jumped out of the truck. Maze did the same.

Kammron stepped forward. He was five-feet-eleven inches tall, caramel-skinned and slim, with deep waves. "Well, well, well, if it isn't the Kings of the Trap. Welcome to Harlem muthafuckas." He laughed and tucked his gun into his belt. "Where the fuck is my money?"

"Yo', we got ya' chips in the truck, nigga. Where the fuck is our people?" I asked, already becoming suspicious of this nigga. As I looked around, I didn't think I saw any place that either Lexi or Hermes could be. That made me nervous. I was starting to think this was maybe a kill mission, where Kammron had brought us all the way out to Harlem so he could dead us. If that was the case, then we had to be the stupidest niggas in the world to walk into a trap like that.

"Whoa, whoa, whoa, this is Harlem. This is my muthafuckin' borough, and in this borough, I call the shots. I run the show. I'll tell you when I'm ready to show you my goods after you show me yours." He laughed and looked back at a few of his homeboys. "Yo', my word, B, you won't believe how many hoes I was able to get to strip just by using those same lines. Shit crazy now that I'm using it for these Brooklyn niggas." He turned back around to face us.

"Nigga, you gotta be out of your mind if you think we're about to give you all of your goods, and you don't show us shit. Fuck you think this is? Bitch, this Red Hook," I said coming closer and dropping two duffel bags in front of him.

"Three million here and three million outside. This gotta be what we show and prove."

"Bitch, huh?" Kammron smirked. He kneeled, his chains clanked into one another. That was the only sound heard throughout the warehouse. He unzipped one of the bags and grabbed a stack of hundreds off the top. He looked it over and nodded. "Look like money, kid. He flipped through it, and sniffed, before replacing the stack, and zipping the bag back. Then he grabbed the other one and with this one, he bypassed the top, and dug all the way to the bottom of it. He pulled up two stacks of cash and sniffed as he flicked through them. He eyed me closely and dropped the money. He stood up. "Yeah, this looks all good, here, Fleet." He replaced the cash and zipped the bag back up. He snapped his fingers and came to a standing position. "Bring that bitch."

Seconds later, a black Chevy Caprice classic drove through the front of the door of the warehouse. It sped and slammed on its brakes directly in front of Kammron. The driver, a heavy-set, dark-skinned dude with Harlem tatted down the sides of each cheek, came and opened the trunk. He yanked a skinny, naked, Hermes out of it and flung her on the ground by Kammron's feet. Then he jumped back in his car and pulled it out of the factory.

Kammron grabbed Hermes by her hair. "Get up, bitch, your brother just saved your life." He flung her over to me.

I caught her in my arms and checked her over for facial scars. "Hermes, sis, are you okay?"

She nodded. "Yeah, I'm good. I feel weak, but I'm good." She closed her eyes and hugged me.

"Can't say I'd pay three million for that, but whatever, to each its own. Where is the rest of my money?" Kammron demanded.

Maze came and dropped two more bags in front of Kammron. "This is the remaining six right here. Where is my daughter?"

"Man, back yo ass up, Fleet? Fuck wrong wit' you?" Kammron pointed the gold gun at Maze.

Maze smacked his lips. "Nigga, fuck you. Where is my Shorty?"

Kammron bent down and followed the same procedure with the bags of money that he'd followed with mine. Then he stood up with a wad of cash in his hand, sniffing it over and over. "Say, B, I think we got a major problem right now." He extended the gun and aimed it at Maze.

Chapter 16

"You see, it's one thing when I rifle through a bag of money, and I can smell that more than half of it is real. That means that you're supposed to be supplying me with three million dollars and that what's in the bag is one point five. That dope addict bitch ain't even worth a hundred grand, so one point five million for her is a steal. I'll accept that, but then, you bitch niggas, come and drop off these bags, and all I'm smelling is heavy ink content, and copy paper. Whoever did ya counterfeiting job needs a lot more work. This is Harlem, bitch, we run every hustle you can imagine. Don't shit get past us, especially not Killa. So, I'ma ask you one time, and keep in mind that your daughter's life depends on it." Kammron stepped forward and aimed his gun at Maze's forehead. "How much money did you bring me, right now?" He cocked the hammer.

Maze was silent. He looked into the barrel of the gun and sucked his teeth. "Take me nigga, and let my baby girl go with, Tyson. I don't give a fuck if you stank me or whatever. Just put my daughter in his arms and let them walk out of here. You can do whatever you want to me."

Kammron shook his head slowly. "N'all, Red Hook, it don't work like that. This shit ain't about you. It's more about Tyson's bitch ass than it is you. He popped me up. Did you forget about that?"

"Man, fuck that, where is my daughter?!" Maze snapped.

"Bitch, where is my cash? How much money total is in those bags?" Kammron placed his finger over the trigger. "I'm not gon' ask you again."

"Three million and a half? But it ain't nothing to get the rest of your cheese. Mafuckas just didn't trust you. You are known for screwing niggas over. Give me my daughter and

I'll make sure you get your two point five million," Maze promised.

Kammron backed up. "Grab these bags! Hurry up!" He said this snapping his fingers. Two members from his crew came and grabbed the bags. They disappeared behind Kammron. "Yo, this is how this is about to go. Instead of you bringing me the two-point-five million that's leftover. Bitch, you, and that fuck nigga right there are going to find my slut for me. Both of you. Find Jazzy and on my borough, I'll release yo' thick ass daughter untouched, well a little touched, did I mention that she is thick?"

Maze rushed him and five of Kammron's security upped two guns apiece on to him. Maze stopped and breathed heavily. "She is eight. How the fuck you gon' say that shit about an eight-year-old?" Maze hollered.

Kammron shrugged his shoulders. "Nigga, I don't know. Maybe it's something in the water, but she sho' don't look no eight, at least not between those lil' thighs of hers." Kammron grabbed his crotch. "Umph."

Maze fell to his knees and lowered his head. "Don't hurt my daughter, man. Please don't hurt my lil' one."

Kammron tossed a cellphone at his feet. "Here, fuck nigga, she on there."

Maze slowly grabbed the phone and looked at the face. He grew weak. "What the fuck? Baby, are you okay?"

I couldn't hear her response but all of a sudden Maze's eyes began to water. He nodded his head and came to his feet. "Daddy about to bring you home, Lexi. I promise I am, and I ain't never gon' let nobody hurt you ever again. Daddy promise."

Kammron kicked the phone out of his hand. "Stop making promises to that baby that you can't keep. I control her destiny, right now. Me, that's it. Me and nobody else. Do you get that?" His face turned into a mask of anger. "Now this is how this is going to work.

"Since you Brooklyn niggas tried to play me. You got forty-eight hours to bring me Jazzy and my money. I need both. If you don't bring me my bitch and my money. Lexi is dead and I'm coming for Brooklyn. Harlem will be all through that bitch with no mercy." He snickered and pulled back the sleeve of his hoodie. He read the time on his Richard Mille.

"The time is eleven fifty-five. You got until Friday this same time to have that bitch and my money. If you don't, you are going to find parts of Lexi all over Brooklyn. Word up, after I thoroughly check her out the right way." He backed up. "Time is ticking, Maze. You can blame this shit on, Tyson, too. He fucked with the wrong nigga. I bet he'll know next time. Coke Kings out." They filed out of the warehouse.

Maze swung at the air twice and fell back to his knees. He broke down crying. "Bitch ass nigga got my baby, man. Why my little girl? She all I got!" He squeezed tears out of his eyes and jumped up with snot running down his nose. He rushed over to me. "Bruh', you gotta press Tasia, she gotta know where her mother is. I know she do.

"Please, man. You heard that nigga. I only got forty-eight hours and he gon' start defiling and cutting up my baby. I need you like I have never needed you before. I am trying to be smooth about the entire situation but help me. I know that's your woman, and you feel some type of way about her. So, I'm going to give you the space to handle this but handle it. And hurry, fuck." He punched his hand and got into the driver's seat.

"Damn, Tyson, I feel like they shoulda let that little girl go and kept me. Kammron was already doing too much to her. His boys did some stuff to me, too, and I hope they got this shit I got. That would be good for their asses? Don't nothing good come from ugliness. Do you think Tasia really knows where Jazzy is?"

"I don't really know, but I guess I'm about to find out," I said leading her into the passenger's seat.

***

"So, you mean to tell me that you expect me to tell you where my mother is? So, you can tell Maze and he can find her, and bring her to Kammron along with three million dollars? So, he can get his daughter back? Tasia asked sitting on the side of the bed next to me two hours later.

"Yeah." I nodded. It was as cut and dry as that.

"And what do you think Kammron is going to do to my mother when he gets his hands on her? Do you have any idea how sick and sadistic that man is? Huh, do you, babe?" She hopped up and started pacing the floor.

"Yo, Hermes said that nigga Kammron was already doing the most to Lexi. She told me that she witnessed some shit that he did that made her sick on the stomach."

"I can imagine. You forget I basically lived with him ever since I was three years old. He didn't wait to go in on me either. Shit, she's lucky she's eight, I was younger than that." She took a deep breath. "Tyson, I understand what that little girl is going through and all of that but this is my mother we're talking about here. I love her, I'm not about to save somebody else's life if it means that she will lose hers. I can't and I won't do it. Now that's just that." She walked out of the room.

I sat on the edge of the bed for a while rubbing my hands together. Then I hopped up with Maze on my mind. I followed her into the kitchen. She was there pouring herself a glass of wine. "Tasia, do you love me?"

She sighed. "More than anything in the world, Tyson."

"Tasia, do you trust me?" I asked, stepping in front of her. She nodded. "Yes, yes, I do. I don't think you can really love somebody without trusting them as well."

I pulled her to me and wrapped my arms around her waist. "Tasia, do you think I would ever do anything to hurt you?" She sat the glass of wine on the table and wrapped her arms around my neck. She looked into my eyes. No, Tyson, I don't think you would. Especially now that I am carrying your seed. Side note, is this the first or second seed of yours?"

"I never asked Ashlynn about that and my mother never spoke about the paternity of Ashlynn's baby. I guess I will find out in time, but, for right now that ain't a worry of mine." I took her small face into my hands and looked into her brown eyes. "Baby, you just said that you loved me more than anything. You also said that you trust me and that you know I will never hurt you, right, baby?"

She popped back on her legs and looked up at me. "Yeah, Daddy, I said that. I mean it, but what are you getting at?"

I leaned into her and kissed her juicy lips. "Boo, I need you to woman up to those words and stand on them. I need you to trust me with Jazzy. I promise you I won't hurt her, and I won't allow death to reach her."

"No, no, no, Daddy. That's my mother. You can't gamble with her. I know Kammron. I know him too well. He is going to kill her. Then he's going to kill me and try his damnest to kill both you and Maze. If I give up where my mother is, she's screwed one by one, just like in a horror movie, then so are we."

I felt myself getting a little angry. I tried as best I could to calm down. "Look, baby, you ain't doing shit but underestimating me. I know what I'm doing. All I wanna do is use your mother as bait so we can get the homey's daughter back. As soon as we get wind of where she is Jazzy can go back into hiding. I'll personally drop her off in Chicago myself. But first thing is first."

"Nope, I love you, but I don't trust it. I care about Maze's daughter, but not more than I care about my mother. You haven't seen some of the ass whippings that I watched, Kammron hand down to her. Some were so brutal I didn't think she was going to get up off the floor. When that Heroin is pumping through his system it's a wrap. He loves and hates my mother at the same time. The fact that she would steal from him and leave means that she doesn't respect him. And when it comes to the king of Harlem which is Kammron his rep and his respect is everything. I still don't understand why he hasn't moved on you for shooting him yet, but you better believe it's coming."

Now I was fuming. "Fuck you think this nigga is God or somethin'? Huh? You don't think these slugs will melt his mafuckin' face away, huh? Man, fuck, Kammron, and fuck your fear of him, too. That bitch nigga got you spooked." I pushed her forehead with my fingers.

She slapped them away and backed up. "Really, Tyson, you're all salty, and shit because I won't let you gamble with my mother's life. What type of shit is that, huh?" She turned her back to me. "Damn, loving yo' ass is a full-time job. You're so fuckin' stubborn. If you don't get your way, then it seems like it's all or nothin'. I hate that."

"Man, fuck what you're saying, right now. There is a baby's life on the line, and you're acting all selfish, and weak. You're about to let bruh's lil' girl die, ain't you? You really are. Your mother every bit in her forties. She done lived a nice life, maybe not a full one, but a nice one, and this baby ain't even had a chance. That's weak, and I am shocked and disappointed in you for taking this route." I pushed her forehead again.

She hauled off and smacked me so hard that my pistol fell out of my waistband and hit the floor. I stumbled back and tasted blood in my mouth. Little stars floated around my head. I swallowed the blood and took a second to gather myself with my eyes closed.

"You gon' stop putting yo lil' funky fingers on me. I know how much you love your mother, and you would never put her under the gun for any reason. You are crazy about that woman. Why is it okay for you to be crazy about your mother, and me not be equally crazy about mine. That doesn't make any fuckin' sense."

I swallowed my blood and mugged her. Her purse was on the table, I grabbed it, and pulled her phone out of it, sliding it into my pocket. "Shorty, I don't give a fuck what you're talking about. I'm your child's father now and we are one. I ain't finna let shit happen to your mother. I got this. Now you ain't gotta have no parts in this endeavor, but I'm finna' snatch up Jazzy and I'm about to use her as bait, so me and the homie can get his daughter back. I need you to trust me and to know that I won't fail you. I know how much she means to you. Please just trust me."

"No girl should have to make these kinds of decisions. Nobody period. I don't understand why my life has to be so hard. This is so unfair." She dropped her head. "And then you took my phone. For what? So, you can go through it to find her. I swear to God I hate this." She walked out of the kitchen in tears. "Tyson, if anything happens to my mother, I will never forgive you. I will never look at you the same. You will have shattered me. So, you better tread smart. Damn, this sucks." She motioned for me to hand her the phone.

I did. "Yo', like I said, all I need is for you to trust me. I ain't gon' let nothing happen to Ms. Jazzy that would devastate you. I got more love for you than that."

Tasia nodded. "I ain't got no other choice than to trust you. It seems like no matter what I do you're going to find a way to get to her anyway. Just please don't make me regret this." She typed some things on the phone and handed it back to me? After she did this she left out of the room and slammed our bedroom door. I could hear her sobbing after the bed squeaked.

Chapter 17

"Say, Tyson, this shit better work, kid. This is my last bit of scratch. If that nigga, Kammron get on that fuck shit and wind up finding a way to take Ms. Jazzy keep Lexi, and take my last lil' three million, Blood, I'ma be sick as hell. I still think we should have gone the other route where we snatched up his people. Made this shit an eye for an eye," Maze said as he drove the Chevy Astro van toward Harlem.

It was ten-thirty, and we were supposed to be meeting Kammron at eleven. I thought it would be smart for us to get a jump on the travel ahead of time, and because of that, we were arriving more than fifteen minutes early.

"We just gotta stick to the game plan. I know everybody's nerves are all over the place. I feel like we're giving dude's ass way too much credit. We gon' stick to the script, and if we see any openings, we gon' dead this nigga, it's as simple as that."

I could feel Ms. Jazzy shivering next to me. She looked out of the window and shook her head. "I still can't believe I'm doing this, Tyson. You know I gotta trust you to allow myself to be used as bait. Lord knows when that man sees me, he is going to kill me dead. I know this. I shoulda taken my ass to Chicago. What the hell am I thinking?" Her teeth began to chatter.

"Ms. Jazzy, be smooth. I ain't gon' let nothin' happen to you that we can't handle. I got this. I got mad love for you, and even more love for Tasia. I know what you mean to her, and I wouldn't devastate her like that. All I need is for you to trust me. Can you do that?"

She smacked her lips. "Boy, what does it look like? I'm here ain't I?" She shook her head and began shaking even harder. "I don't know why I'm here? I think it's stupid. But as long as Kammron is breathing and roaming around New York,

I'm going to have to fear for my life. I'd rather get this thing over and done with."

"That's the right attitude, Ms. Jazzy, straight up. We gon' get this nigga. He ain't invincible." Maze looked over his shoulder at her. "But yo, are you really telling the truth about all that money that you robbed his ass for? Did you really already have it put in the bank and separated into multiple accounts?"

I knew she was lying, but I didn't want Maze to get wind of that. The only way I was able to get her to roll with us is to promise that she would be able to keep the money she'd hit the Coke Kings for. Also that she would be able to keep her life and Kammron would lose his. As a man, I didn't know for certain if I could keep either of the last two promises, but I was going to try as hard as I could to do just that.

"Tyson, you said I didn't have to keep explaining the money situation. Can you please tell Maze to ease up? Damn. Shit is already grim enough. I don't need to be attacked by y'all, too." She didn't even bother to look up at Maze.

"Yo', Maze, what the fuck, B? Leave her alone. We ain't gon' lose ya scratch. Trust me on that, damn!" I hollered at him.

"We've been in the streets grinding hard, Tyson. I can't have that shit being for nothing. Mafuckas been trying to take our heads off every single day. This money is all I got to show for our hustle, kid. It ain't much, but we never thought we would ever get to see millions growing up in Brooklyn. Now that I got them bitches, I don't want to lose them."

"Boy, what about your daughter, huh? What about, Lexi? You thank she worth more than a few million that you were able to come up with in less than a year?" Ms. Jazzy asked him.

Maze didn't respond right away. After a moment, he cleared his throat, then eyed her in his rearview mirror. "First of all, it ain't a few million. It was four in all. A million last time and three this time. And, of course, my daughter is worth more than money. That's the love of my life." He frowned. "Don't try and make it seem like I don't love my daughter more than money? That shit weak, Jazzy, word up."

"I'm just saying, it seems like everybody has something at stake here. You're not the only one, but you're doing a lot of complaining. So, baby please, knock it off." She rolled her eyes.

Maze grunted. "Yo', I don't know what it is about you and your daughter, Tasia but both of you bitches get on my nerves. Straight up. Had it not been for, Tyson I would have smacked fire from y'all."

"Maze, chill, B. It's all good. We gotta stay focused, we aren't the enemy. That nigga, Kammron is," I reminded him.

"Yeah, well, let Jazzy know that. That bitch getting on my nerves trying to make it seem like I don't love my daughter more than money. Anybody else says some dumb shit like that to me and they getting smoked like a Dutch." He mugged her through the mirror again. "Yo', and, Tyson, ain't got shit to lose in this whole thing no more either." He looked over at me. "Blood already got his sister back, and his bitch at home. I don't know how much you mean to him, but I ain't seeing that you'd be that much of a loss." He curled his upper lip. "Since we stating facts and all of that."

Ms. Jazzy looked over at me, I could tell that she was worried. "Damn, I never thought about it like that. Now you got my mind all messed up, Maze." She looked out the window, then back at me. "Tyson, you got me, right? I mean you're not going to allow anything to happen to me, are you?"

I'd never seen a female look more vulnerable in my life. The look she gave me made me downright sad because I knew I didn't have all the answers, and I didn't know for sure that I was going to be able to save her and help her walk back out of this meeting alive. I didn't know what Kammron had up his sleeve. I didn't even have a clear picture in my mind as to how we were going to go about everything. I became nervous, but I put on a brave face.

"I got you, mama. I ain't gon' let shit happen to you. You know how I get down out here. You know how much I care about you and Tasia." I kissed her cheek. "You said you trusted me, right?"

She smiled, even though I could feel that she was shaking like crazy. "Yeah, baby, I do. I swear I do." She exhaled loudly. "I just wanna get all this over with. Once this shit is behind me, I won't have to worry about Kammron no more. You promised me that too, baby, right?"

I swallowed my spit, once again, I was unsure, but I had to make it seem like I had it all figured out. "Yes. This is going to be a clean slate. Once again, I got you."

"Okay." Ms. Jazzy smiled and leaned into me. "I hope you don't think just because you're saving me from this monster I'm going to give you any of my money, Tyson, because I just might not." She looked out of the window as we began to drive through the slums of Harlem. "You have no idea how much pain and suffering I've gone through with this man, ever since I've been with him. The things I've caught him doing to my daughter and the ways that he's broken both of us down has been enough to drive any woman crazy. All I've gotten to pay his ass back is the little money that I kept over the years. I plan to live out the rest of my life happily. No woman should allow any man to break her down in the way that Kammron did me." She closed her eyes. "He started defiling my daughter before she was even old enough to understand what all that stuff was. He took her innocence, and ever since, I've never been able to love myself. I have hated the reflection I see looking back in the mirror, even to this day." Tears seeped out of her closed eyelids.

I pulled her closer to me and tightened my arm around her body. "I'm sorry that you had to go through that, Ms. Jazzy. That nigga Kammron deserves every bit of what he's about to get." I kissed her cheek and kept my lips there. "Had I known 'bout this a long time ago, I would have been smoked him. Women are to be protected, and cherished. Any nigga that don't follow that game plan, especially when it comes to our sisters, needs to be slumped. Straight up."

Maze drove past Frederick Douglass Boulevard and adjusted the Tech on his lap. "Yo', if that sick as nigga put his hands on my seed, B, I swear to God, I'ma torture and kill his ass. I can't imagine Lexi going through whatever he put those bitches through. That'll be fucked up, damn."

"Excuse you, Maze," Ms. Jazzy, busted out.

"What?" Maze looked over his shoulder at us. I was mugging his goofy ass and shaking my head. "What?" he asked again.

"Can you have some compassion for anybody else that's outside of your situation? Jesus Christ." She rolled her eyes.

"What, are you talking about now?" Maze wanted to know, oblivious to his levels of disrespect.

"Bruh, she just revealed some deep, dark, things to us without actually going into detail, but one can only imagine, and instead of you either keeping ya mouth closed and shaking ya head, you chose to follow up and call both of these sistas bitches. That's foul, bruh. Now ain't the time for that shit," I said irritated at him.

"Damn, nigga, my bad. Y'all acting sensitive as a muthafucka. But you know what I mean. Anyway, let's get this shit over and done with so I can get my seed back. I need a mafuckin' vacation. Word up."

I kissed Ms. Jazzy's cheek and kept my lips there. "It's all good, Goddess. I'm sorry for what you had to go through. I'ma make sure you never have to worry about that again." I held her closer to me and rocked from side to side slightly until we pulled back up at the factory from the previous time.

Chapter 18

Kammron stood in red and black fatigues with a black half-mask across his face, and bullets lined around his left shoulder as if he were Rambo or something. Behind him, stood Bonkers and six three hundred plus pound dudes. They all had on the same color fatigues as Kammron. When we drove further into the factory, Maze stopped just in front of the door and threw the van in park. Kammron stayed still. Ms. Jazzy was shaking so bad, I could hear her teeth chattering together.

I kissed her forehead, and pushed her to the ground of the van, before hopping out, along with Maze. I grabbed one of the duffle bags and Maze grabbed the other two. I stepped in front of the van and dropped my bag.

"Say, Blood, we got everything we are supposed to have. Mafuckas just wanna end this whole thing right here, and right now. From here on out, you stay in Harlem, and we'll stay out the way back in Red Hook."

Kammron stepped forward and proceeded to walk over to me. "You see, that's the thang, though. If you punk mafuckas would have stayed in your own lane in the first place. We wouldn't be having this meeting, nor this war that seems like is on the edge of brewing. Mafuckas shouldn't worry about what I do wit' my bitches. My hoes are mine, and they ain't of no concern to you, or nobody else. At least they shouldn't be. But you captain save-a-ho ass niggas had to get in my bidness."

"Fuck you talking about, Blood, I ain't jumped in shit? I don't give a fuck' about no bitch. You didn't have no right bringing my little girl into this shit. And speaking of her, where is she?"

Kammron looked from his right to left, then back over to us. He made it seem like he was trying to see past us. "Yo, I know this goofy ain't asking me for his jewel? When I don't see the bitch nor money I asked for nowhere near me. How 'bout you run what the fuck you owe Killa, and we'll see 'bout that lil' ho in the making you asking me 'bout." He pulled his nose.

"Blood, watch yo' mouth when it comes to my seed. She's just a baby," Maze started.

Kammron waved him off. "Shut that emotional shit up. Ain't nobody trying to hear that. Fuck is my shit at?"

I tossed him the first duffel bag. "Huh, that's a million. All cash, no cap."

"Whoopty do, it better be. Y'all ain't got no more room for error, Tyson. This shit better be correct. Else I'ma find out which one of you mafuckas is the weakest link, and bye-bye yo' ass." He kneeled down and unzipped the bag. He dug his hand inside and pulled out two stacks of cash. He sniffed them and flipped through the bills. Then he replaced them and dug all the way to the bottom and repeated the process. He nodded. "This is valid. Tuck this bag, Fleet."

Bonkers picked up the duffle and walked back to the Range Rover that was parked a few feet away from them. He threw the bag in the passenger's seat and closed the door. He appeared to be about five-feet-ten, brown-skinned, with long dreads, and muscles. "Where the rest of it at, Kammron? I thought you said it was supposed to be three million?"

Kammron ignored him. He mugged Maze. "You got something for me, nigga?"

Maze tossed the remaining duffle bags at Kammron's feet. "That's the rest. It's a million in each. That's the three million that Jazzy owed you. And we got her in the van. Where is my shorty?"

Kammron sniffed through the money and kept Maze waiting to hear his response to his questioning. He picked up stack after stack, sniffing it with a frown on his face. Finally, he smiled, after zipping the bags up and handing them to, Bonkers. "Seems like this meeting is going well so far. What else y'all got for me?"

"n'all fuck that, nigga. Where is the homey's daughter at?" I stepped up to Kammron. "We ain't finna' keep giving you all of what we got, and you ain't giving us shit."

Kammron swung so fast that it caught me off guard. He bust me right in the mouth and swung again and caught me on the jaw knocking me to one knee. I swallowed my blood before it fell to the concrete. I didn't know what kind of a murder scene was about to be left at this warehouse but I didn't want any traces of my DNA left behind.

Kammron stood over me. "New Jack ass, nigga, fuck you think you calling shots for? That ain't how this shit go. Bitch, you're in Harlem. Home of the Coke Kings. I run this shit, not a Brooklyn nigga."

Maze came and helped me to my feet. "Come on, Tyson. That was some snake shit. Don't even trip, Blood."

I slowly made my way back over to our side with my heart pounding. Allowing Kammron to put his hands on me, and not react right away, was the hardest thing I felt like I had ever had to do in my entire life. But I did it, I swallowed my blood and steadied myself.

"Bring that lil' bitch out so this fuck nigga can see her," Kammron ordered.

Bonkers disappeared into the Range Rover. When he came back out, he had a handful of Lexi's hair. He brought her beside Kammron and held her there. It hurt my heart because she was dressed in nothing but a pair of panties. Kammron didn't even have the decency to allow her to wear a shirt. I think that this was a direct shot to Maze's mind, because as soon as Lexi was brought out that way, Kammron's men upped their assault rifles, and aimed them at us.

Maze fell to his knees. "Baby." His eyes watered. "My precious baby."

Kammron yanked her back by her hair. "Come here, bitch."

"Ahhhhh!" she screamed, before falling on the ground beside him.

Maze jumped up and got ready to rush over toward Kammron. "Muthafucka."

I grabbed him back. "Chill, bruh, just relax."

Kammron laughed. "Yeah, nigga, listen to that bitch ass nigga I just punched in the mouth. Let him speak some sense into yo' silly ass." He looked down at Lexi. "Now where is, Jazzy?"

Maze shook me off him and jogged to the van. He slid open the side door. "Come on, Shorty. We're doing this shit, right now. Come on."

All I saw was, Jazzy's feet kicking at him. "No, no, Tyson! Tyson, come get this crazy-ass boy!"

Kammron laughed. "Aw yeah, that's my bitch's voice. I know it anywhere." He headed over to the van with two of his henchmen walking behind him on security. When he got by me, he bumped me out of the way. "Move nigga."

I stumbled back and caught my footing. "Here he comes, Ms. Jazzy, just do what he says. Please."

She continued to kick at Maze. "Get off me, Maze. I'm not doing this anymore! Tyson! Tyson! Baby, what's going on?!"

Maze jumped back. "Man, fuck that crazy bitch. Kammron, you deal with her."

Kammron laughed. "Fuck out my way, nigga." He flung Maze to the side. Maze fell next to me. Kammron dusted off his clothes and stepped up to the side door where Ms. Jazzy was. "Say, baby, why are you taking me through all this? All I wanna do is put our happy family back together, is that so wrong?" He stuck his head inside of the door.

"Rest in hell, Kammron!" *Boom! Boom! Boom! Boom!* Bullet after bullet ripped into Kammron's chest. He flew back shaking from side to side before he wound up on his ass. As soon as he hit the dirt I upped and popped both of his security twice in the back of the head while they were looking down at a bleeding Kammron. They slumped and fell on top of him, with their brains leaking out the front of their faces, and smoke coming out of the holes that I'd created.

Maze grabbed his Tech off the passenger's seat where he'd placed it for easy access, and let that bitch ride back-to-back? *Blocka! Blocka! Blocka! Blocka!* Fire spit from his gun rapidly. "Bitch ass niggas!"

Bonkers grabbed Lexi and rushed to the truck with her. He threw her inside of it and hopped behind the steering wheel, just as the windshield shattered. He threw the truck in drive and stepped on the gas.

Maze ran at him bussing back-to-back. His bullets ate at the driver's side. Bonkers returned fire. Maze kept shooting. I joined in. Maze ran at the truck, gunning like crazy. The Coke Kings' remaining security had already retreated in the other truck leaving both Kammron and Bonkers to fend for themselves.

Maze kept shooting. Ms. Jazzy stumbled out of the van and looked down at Kammron. She had tears in her eyes. Bonkers sped out of the warehouse and suddenly slammed on his brakes while Maze stopped to reload his gun. I heard a gunshot and then the driver's door to Bonkers' truck opened. He slung Lexi out of it and drove off. She rolled twice and lay flat on her back with her eyes wide open.

"Nooooooo!" Maze ran to her at full speed.

Before he could get to her, three Suburban trucks pulled up with their doors opened. They slammed on their brakes and I saw what seemed like twenty nappy dreaded Jamaicans jump out of the trucks with assault rifles in their hands. They kneeled on the ground and aimed their weapons at us.

King walked around them and stopped directly in front of the first Suburban. He ran his finger across his neck. "Ya' dare' go against dis' ear legacy boi. Ya' cum down dare and lose what ya Dunn' gained. Die, moi denounce yer' blood. Fire!" He stepped back, and the shots began to ring out rapidly.

To Be Continued...
King of the Trap 3
Coming Soon

Submission Guideline

Submit the first three chapters of your completed manuscript to ldpsubmissions@gmail.com, subject line: Your book's title. The manuscript must be in a .doc file and sent as an attachment. Document should be in Times New Roman, double spaced and in size 12 font. Also, provide your synopsis and full contact information. If sending multiple submissions, they must each be in a separate email.

Have a story but no way to send it electronically? You can still submit to LDP/Ca$h Presents. Send in the first three chapters, written or typed, of your completed manuscript to:

LDP: Submissions Dept
Po Box 944
Stockbridge, Ga 30281

DO NOT send original manuscript. Must be a duplicate.

Provide your synopsis and a cover letter containing your full contact information.

Thanks for considering LDP and Ca$h Presents.

T.J. Edwards

Coming Soon from Lock Down Publications/Ca$h Presents

BOW DOWN TO MY GANGSTA

By **Ca$h**

TORN BETWEEN TWO

By **Coffee**

THE STREETS STAINED MY SOUL **II**

By **Marcellus Allen**

BLOOD OF A BOSS **VI**

SHADOWS OF THE GAME II

TRAP BASTARD II

By **Askari**

LOYAL TO THE GAME **IV**

By **T.J. & Jelissa**

IF LOVING YOU IS WRONG... **III**

By **Jelissa**

TRUE SAVAGE **VIII**

MIDNIGHT CARTEL IV

DOPE BOY MAGIC IV

CITY OF KINGZ III

By **Chris Green**

BLAST FOR ME **III**

A SAVAGE DOPEBOY III

CUTTHROAT MAFIA III

DUFFLE BAG CARTEL VI

HEARTLESS GOON VI

By **Ghost**

A HUSTLER'S DECEIT III

KILL ZONE **II**

BAE BELONGS TO ME III

A DOPE BOY'S QUEEN III

By **Aryanna**

COKE KINGS V

KING OF THE TRAP III

By **T.J. Edwards**

GORILLAZ IN THE BAY V

3X KRAZY III

De'Kari

THE STREETS ARE CALLING II

Duquie Wilson

KINGPIN KILLAZ IV

STREET KINGS III

PAID IN BLOOD III

CARTEL KILLAZ IV

DOPE GODS III

Hood Rich

SINS OF A HUSTLA II

ASAD

KINGZ OF THE GAME VI

Playa Ray

SLAUGHTER GANG IV

RUTHLESS HEART IV

By Willie Slaughter

FUK SHYT II

By Blakk Diamond

TRAP QUEEN

By Troublesome

YAYO V

GHOST MOB II

Stilloan Robinson

KINGPIN DREAMS III

By Paper Boi Rari

CREAM II

By Yolanda Moore

SON OF A DOPE FIEND III

By Renta

FOREVER GANGSTA II

GLOCKS ON SATIN SHEETS III

By Adrian Dulan

LOYALTY AIN'T PROMISED III

By Keith Williams

THE PRICE YOU PAY FOR LOVE III

By Destiny Skai

I'M NOTHING WITHOUT HIS LOVE II

SINS OF A THUG II

By Monet Dragun

LIFE OF A SAVAGE IV

MURDA SEASON IV

GANGLAND CARTEL IV

CHI'RAQ GANGSTAS IV

KILLERS ON ELM STREET II

JACK BOYZ N DA BRONX II

By **Romell Tukes**

QUIET MONEY IV

EXTENDED CLIP III

THUG LIFE IV

By **Trai'Quan**

THE STREETS MADE ME III

By **Larry D. Wright**

IF YOU CROSS ME ONCE II

ANGEL III

By **Anthony Fields**

FRIEND OR FOE III

By **Mimi**

SAVAGE STORMS III

By **Meesha**

BLOOD ON THE MONEY III

By J-Blunt

THE STREETS WILL NEVER CLOSE II

By K'ajji

NIGHTMARES OF A HUSTLA III

By King Dream

IN THE ARM OF HIS BOSS

By Jamila

MONEY, MURDER & MEMORIES III

Malik D. Rice

CONCRETE KILLAZ II

By Kingpen

T.J. Edwards

HARD AND RUTHLESS II
By Von Wiley Hall
LEVELS TO THIS SHYT II
By Ah'Million
MOB TIES II
By SayNoMore
BODYMORE MURDERLAND II
By Delmont Player
THE LAST OF THE OGS II
Tranay Adams
FOR THE LOVE OF A BOSS II
By C. D. Blue

<u>**Available Now**</u>

RESTRAINING ORDER **I & II**
By **CA$H & Coffee**
LOVE KNOWS NO BOUNDARIES **I II & III**
By **Coffee**
RAISED AS A GOON I, II, III & IV
BRED BY THE SLUMS I, II, III
BLAST FOR ME I & II
ROTTEN TO THE CORE I II III
A BRONX TALE I, II, III
DUFFLE BAG CARTEL I II III IV V

HEARTLESS GOON I II III IV V

A SAVAGE DOPEBOY I II

DRUG LORDS I II III

CUTTHROAT MAFIA I II

By **Ghost**

LAY IT DOWN **I & II**

LAST OF A DYING BREED I II

BLOOD STAINS OF A SHOTTA I & II III

By **Jamaica**

LOYAL TO THE GAME I II III

LIFE OF SIN I, II III

By **TJ & Jelissa**

BLOODY COMMAS I & II

SKI MASK CARTEL I II & III

KING OF NEW YORK I II,III IV V

RISE TO POWER I II III

COKE KINGS I II III IV

BORN HEARTLESS I II III IV

KING OF THE TRAP I II

By **T.J. Edwards**

IF LOVING HIM IS WRONG…I & II

LOVE ME EVEN WHEN IT HURTS I II III

By **Jelissa**

WHEN THE STREETS CLAP BACK I & II III

THE HEART OF A SAVAGE I II III

By **Jibril Williams**

A DISTINGUISHED THUG STOLE MY HEART I II & III

T.J. Edwards

LOVE SHOULDN'T HURT I II III IV
RENEGADE BOYS I II III IV
PAID IN KARMA I II III
SAVAGE STORMS I II
By **Meesha**
A GANGSTER'S CODE I &, II III
A GANGSTER'S SYN I II III
THE SAVAGE LIFE I II III
CHAINED TO THE STREETS I II III
BLOOD ON THE MONEY I II
By J-Blunt
PUSH IT TO THE LIMIT
By **Bre' Hayes**
BLOOD OF A BOSS **I, II, III, IV, V**
SHADOWS OF THE GAME
TRAP BASTARD
By **Askari**
THE STREETS BLEED MURDER **I, II & III**
THE HEART OF A GANGSTA I II& III
By **Jerry Jackson**
CUM FOR ME I II III IV V VI
An **LDP Erotica Collaboration**
BRIDE OF A HUSTLA **I II & II**
THE FETTI GIRLS **I, II& III**
CORRUPTED BY A GANGSTA I, II III, IV
BLINDED BY HIS LOVE
THE PRICE YOU PAY FOR LOVE I II

152

King of the Trap 2

DOPE GIRL MAGIC I II III

By **Destiny Skai**

WHEN A GOOD GIRL GOES BAD

By **Adrienne**

THE COST OF LOYALTY I II III

By Kweli

A GANGSTER'S REVENGE **I II III & IV**

THE BOSS MAN'S DAUGHTERS I II III IV V

A SAVAGE LOVE **I & II**

BAE BELONGS TO ME I II

A HUSTLER'S DECEIT I, II, III

WHAT BAD BITCHES DO I, II, III

SOUL OF A MONSTER I II III

KILL ZONE

A DOPE BOY'S QUEEN I II

By **Aryanna**

A KINGPIN'S AMBITON

A KINGPIN'S AMBITION **II**

I MURDER FOR THE DOUGH

By **Ambitious**

TRUE SAVAGE I II III IV V VI VII

DOPE BOY MAGIC I, II, III

MIDNIGHT CARTEL I II III

CITY OF KINGZ I II

By **Chris Green**

A DOPEBOY'S PRAYER

By **Eddie "Wolf" Lee**

THE KING CARTEL **I, II & III**

By **Frank Gresham**

THESE NIGGAS AIN'T LOYAL **I, II & III**

By **Nikki Tee**

GANGSTA SHYT **I II &III**

By **CATO**

THE ULTIMATE BETRAYAL

By **Phoenix**

BOSS'N UP **I , II & III**

By **Royal Nicole**

I LOVE YOU TO DEATH

By Destiny J

I RIDE FOR MY HITTA

I STILL RIDE FOR MY HITTA

By **Misty Holt**

LOVE & CHASIN' PAPER

By **Qay Crockett**

TO DIE IN VAIN

SINS OF A HUSTLA

By **ASAD**

BROOKLYN HUSTLAZ

By **Boogsy Morina**

BROOKLYN ON LOCK I & II

By **Sonovia**

GANGSTA CITY

By **Teddy Duke**

A DRUG KING AND HIS DIAMOND I & II III

King of the Trap 2

A DOPEMAN'S RICHES

HER MAN, MINE'S TOO I, II

CASH MONEY HO'S

THE WIFEY I USED TO BE I II

By Nicole Goosby

TRAPHOUSE KING **I II & III**

KINGPIN KILLAZ I II III

STREET KINGS I II

PAID IN BLOOD **I II**

CARTEL KILLAZ I II III

DOPE GODS I II

By **Hood Rich**

LIPSTICK KILLAH **I, II, III**

CRIME OF PASSION I II & III

FRIEND OR FOE I II

By **Mimi**

STEADY MOBBN' **I, II, III**

THE STREETS STAINED MY SOUL

By **Marcellus Allen**

WHO SHOT YA **I, II, III**

SON OF A DOPE FIEND I II

Renta

GORILLAZ IN THE BAY **I II III IV**

TEARS OF A GANGSTA I II

3X KRAZY I II

DE'KARI

TRIGGADALE I II III

T.J. Edwards

Elijah R. Freeman
GOD BLESS THE TRAPPERS I, II, III
THESE SCANDALOUS STREETS I, II, III
FEAR MY GANGSTA I, II, III IV, V
THESE STREETS DON'T LOVE NOBODY I, II
BURY ME A G I, II, III, IV, V
A GANGSTA'S EMPIRE I, II, III, IV
THE DOPEMAN'S BODYGAURD I II
THE REALEST KILLAZ I II III
THE LAST OF THE OGS
Tranay Adams
THE STREETS ARE CALLING
Duquie Wilson
MARRIED TO A BOSS... I II III
By Destiny Skai & Chris Green
KINGZ OF THE GAME I II III IV V
Playa Ray
SLAUGHTER GANG I II III
RUTHLESS HEART I II III
By Willie Slaughter
FUK SHYT
By Blakk Diamond
DON'T F#CK WITH MY HEART I II
By Linnea
ADDICTED TO THE DRAMA I II III
IN THE ARM OF HIS BOSS II
By Jamila

YAYO I II III IV

A SHOOTER'S AMBITION I II

By S. Allen

TRAP GOD I II III

By Troublesome

FOREVER GANGSTA

GLOCKS ON SATIN SHEETS I II

By Adrian Dulan

TOE TAGZ I II III

LEVELS TO THIS SHYT

By Ah'Million

KINGPIN DREAMS I II

By Paper Boi Rari

CONFESSIONS OF A GANGSTA I II III

By Nicholas Lock

I'M NOTHING WITHOUT HIS LOVE

SINS OF A THUG

By Monet Dragun

CAUGHT UP IN THE LIFE I II III

By Robert Baptiste

NEW TO THE GAME I II III

MONEY, MURDER & MEMORIES I II

By **Malik D. Rice**

LIFE OF A SAVAGE I II III

A GANGSTA'S QUR'AN I II III

MURDA SEASON I II III

GANGLAND CARTEL I II III

T.J. Edwards

CHI'RAQ GANGSTAS I II III
KILLERS ON ELM STREET
JACK BOYZ N DA BRONX
By **Romell Tukes**
LOYALTY AIN'T PROMISED I II
By Keith Williams
QUIET MONEY I II III
THUG LIFE I II III
EXTENDED CLIP I II
By **Trai'Quan**
THE STREETS MADE ME I II
By **Larry D. Wright**
THE ULTIMATE SACRIFICE I, II, III, IV, V, VI
KHADIFI
IF YOU CROSS ME ONCE
ANGEL I II
By **Anthony Fields**
THE LIFE OF A HOOD STAR
By Ca$h & Rashia Wilson
THE STREETS WILL NEVER CLOSE
By K'ajji
CREAM
By Yolanda Moore
NIGHTMARES OF A HUSTLA I II
By King Dream
CONCRETE KILLAZ
By Kingpen

HARD AND RUTHLESS

By Von Wiley Hall

GHOST MOB II

Stilloan Robinson

MOB TIES

By SayNoMore

BODYMORE MURDERLAND

By Delmont Player

FOR THE LOVE OF A BOSS

By C. D. Blue

BOOKS BY LDP'S CEO, CA$H

TRUST IN NO MAN

TRUST IN NO MAN 2

TRUST IN NO MAN 3

BONDED BY BLOOD

SHORTY GOT A THUG

THUGS CRY

THUGS CRY 2

THUGS CRY 3

TRUST NO BITCH

TRUST NO BITCH 2

TRUST NO BITCH 3

TIL MY CASKET DROPS

RESTRAINING ORDER

RESTRAINING ORDER 2

IN LOVE WITH A CONVICT

LIFE OF A HOOD STAR